RYAN RETRIBUTION
NEW YORK RUTHLESS: BOOK 3

SADIE KINCAID

RED HOUSE PRESS

NEW YORK RUTHLESS

Ryan Retribution is book 3 in the New York Ruthless series. It is a dark Mafia, reverse harem romance which deals with adult themes which may be triggering for some, as well as scenes of a violent and sexual nature.

If you haven't read books 1 and 2 in the series yet, you can find them on Amazon
    Ryan Rule
    Ryan Redemption

For all of you Ryan fans! Thank you for everything xx

CHAPTER
ONE

JESSIE

S hane jumps off the bed as Mikey and Conor rush into the room.

"They took Liam?" he snarls. "What the fuck happened?"

Mikey shakes his head, looking too distraught to speak. Conor places his hand on Mikey's shoulder and answers Shane's question. "Liam was obviously the target. They distracted Mikey and me with some phony bullshit, and they took him, Shane. He was throwing a couple of underage college kids out and they pulled up in a van and grabbed him."

I sit up and stare at Conor, my mouth hanging open and my stomach twisted in a knot of anxiety as I think about Liam and what they're doing to him right now.

"Did anyone see who took him. Did they get the plates?" Shane growls.

Conor shakes his head. "By the time the bouncers saw what was happening, it was too late to get the plates. All they saw was a black van. Couldn't even be sure of the model."

"They'll probably be stolen anyway. But it will be on CCTV,

1

right?" I ask as I climb out of bed, the adrenaline kicking in and jumpstarting my brain.

"Yeah," Conor says with a nod.

"Good. I can access the traffic cameras and track the van's movements," I say, pulling on a pair of sweatpants.

"You said the Russians took him? How do you know that if nobody saw anything?" Shane asks as he rubs a hand across his jaw and steps closer to Mikey, who is so pale, he looks like he's about to pass out.

"Who the fuck else would it be?" Mikey stares blankly at him.

I swallow the surge of guilt that pulses through my chest. If I hadn't come back, Liam would still be here.

"This isn't on you, Jessie," Conor says softly, as though he's reading my mind.

"He's right. But we don't have time to think about anything right now except for finding Liam," Shane barks as he gives Mikey a brief hug before whispering something in his ear that seems to snap him from his daze. "Were the college kids in on it?" he asks, turning back to Conor.

"Maybe. But they're long gone. There was another woman with a kid who was asking for me. She must have been in on it, but we didn't realize that and she's in the wind now too."

"Fuck!" Shane hisses.

"We still got the guy with the Mohawk though," Mikey adds.

"The Mohawk?" Shane and I say in unison.

"Some kid with green hair told me that Jessie wanted to see me in the VIP area. That was how they distracted me," Mikey replies.

Shane nods before looking at Conor. "Let's go make this kid talk then," he says and Conor nods his understanding. Then

Shane turns to me. "Jessie, do your thing, sweetheart, and find out where they've taken our boy."

"Of course. I'm on it."

"You think you can help Jessie out, kid?" Shane says to Mikey.

"Yeah. We'll get him back, won't we, Shane?" he asks, sounding like a scared little boy, and my heart breaks for him.

"Course we will, kid," Shane replies as he pulls him into a brief hug. "But we need to move. Now."

"Yeah," Mikey nods as he struggles to compose himself.

Shane gives me a final glance, his face full of emotion, before he heads out the door with Conor hot on his heels. When they're gone, I turn to look at their younger brother. He stares at me, his face blank and his deep brown eyes vacant. "Come on," I hold out my hand to him. "We've got work to do."

He takes my hand and I wrap my fingers around his tightly. The Ryan brothers have never needed me quite so much as they do right now, and I am determined not to let them down. Not to let Liam down. The thought of anything happening to him — of him not coming back here, it is unthinkable. So, I don't think about it. I push it to the back of my mind and focus on what I need to do to find him.

I FIRE up the computer in Shane's office while Mikey hovers nervously behind me. Anxiety and fear radiate from him in waves. "Hey," I turn to him. "I might need to run a few programs at the same time here. So, can you bring me every laptop and every tablet in this apartment while I make a start?"

He stares blankly at me for a second, but then he nods his head. "Yeah. Sure. All of them?"

"Every single device you can find."

He straightens his shoulders and sucks in a deep breath. "Of course, Red."

"Before you go. Can you remember what time it was when you last saw Liam?"

He swallows hard, and I have no doubt that he is wondering if it will have been the last time he ever saw his twin alive, because I can't help thinking it too. "Yeah. It was a quarter after one." Then he marches out of the room full of purpose and I turn back to the screen and enter the password before it flickers to life.

I bring up the club security footage first and switch to the camera on the street outside where Liam was taken. I go back over an hour to just before 1am and scan the screen for signs of a black van. At 1:20am, Liam appears on the screen with two scantily dressed females. The sight of him makes my heart start to pound in my chest and I sit up straight and take a deep breath. I cannot let my emotions get the better of me right now. I work best when I can be detached and have a clear head, and Liam needs me at my best. He deserves me at my best. Both of the women appear drunk as they stumble onto the pavement. Liam holds his arm out to catch one before she face-plants the concrete and the other clings onto his arm. They all have their backs to the camera so I can't see their faces, but I can pull footage from inside the club if we need to trace them.

I watch as Liam guides them to a cab parked out front, before he opens the door and they stumble through it and onto the back seat. Liam watches the cab drive away and then he turns around, and for a brief couple of seconds I see his face on the screen and have to remind myself not to think about what he might be going through right now. It seems like he is about to walk back into the club, but then he disappears and the street is empty.

I blink at the screen in confusion before rewinding it back.

4

But the same thing happens. One second Liam is there, and the next he's gone. I rewind it again and check the time stamp, and it's only then that I realize that two minutes have been completely erased.

Damn! Someone has hacked into the security system. My heart sinks. If they were good enough to do that and erase just the specific time that he was taken, then no doubt they have messed with the footage from the other cameras too. I rewind again and notice that the cut is almost seamless. If someone wasn't looking closely, then it would appear that Liam came back into the club. So, we are definitely dealing with someone who knows what they're doing, and that makes my stomach twist into a knot, because it means it's going to take me much longer to track him than I thought.

Mikey comes back into the office carrying five laptops, and places them on the desk. "We got some tablets too somewhere. Should I go find them?" he asks.

I shake my head. We do need the extra computers, but the task of finding every device was also a distraction technique to give Mikey something useful to do. Now I need him. "No. I want you to turn all of them on so I can run some different software. I also need you to use one to check the security footage in the alleyway where Conor was, and also inside the club from 1am to about 1:30. Look for anything suspicious, or anything that will give us a clue who took Liam. And could you also check if there are any time lapses or footage missing?"

Mikey frowns at me. "They fucked with our security feed?"

"Yes. But I have plenty of other feeds to tap into along this street. Don't worry."

Mikey nods and picks up a laptop before sitting on the chair opposite me, and we both get to work.

TWO

Conor and I stand in the elevator in silence as it takes us down to the basement, where some of our bouncers are holding the guy with the green Mohawk. I feel the worry and the anger in my brother and it echoes mine. Of all of us, why choose Liam? He's probably the strongest of us physically, but emotionally, he's the most vulnerable. He's so much like our mother — quiet and thoughtful. Mikey has always had a big mouth and used his sense of humor as a distraction. But Liam was always quiet. As a kid, he would sit there and take whatever our father doled out. My heart breaks inside as I think about what he endured as a child and the man he has become in spite of it.

My fists are clenched at my sides as the elevator comes to a stop and Conor and I step out.

"Have you spoken to this guy at all?"

"Yeah," Conor says as we make our way toward the small room near the back. "But it was real quick. He said he didn't know anything and was only doing what this girl asked him to."

I nod as we reach the steel door and our bouncer opens it so we can walk inside. Sitting in the middle of the room, strapped to a chair, is a kid in his early twenties, with a neon green Mohawk. He has duct tape over his mouth, a busted nose, a huge gash above his eye that's causing blood to run down his face, and a piss stain on the crotch of his stonewash jeans.

Chester, one of our bouncers, is standing beside him silently. Chester won't have touched him, because he would've been told not to by Conor or Mikey, so I wonder which of my brothers is responsible for his face. I could rip this guy's head off his neck right now, given the mood I'm in, but I need to know what he knows.

"Take off the tape," I say to Chester, who complies immediately, making the kid wince in pain. "Out," I indicate the door and Chester nods his understanding before leaving Conor and me alone.

The kid in the chair stares up at us, his lip trembling and his body shivering. At least he has the good sense to stay quiet.

"What were you doing in our club?" I ask.

He blinks at me, his mouth opening and closing like a fish in a tank.

Conor raises his foot and kicks the kid in the kneecap, making him surge forward as he howls in pain, but he is restrained with chains and he falls back against the chair, his head hanging limply against his chest. "My brother just asked you a question, asshole!" Conor hisses.

The kid lifts his head and looks at us. "I was there with my girlfriend."

"Where's your girlfriend now?" I ask him.

"We had a fight. She went home hours ago." He is crying now. "I don't know anything. I swear."

"I think we'll be the judge of that," I snarl.

I nod to Conor and he walks behind the chair and holds the kid's head up by his hair. "What's your name?" I ask.

"Henry Campbell," he sniffs.

"Well, Henry. I am going to ask you some questions, and every time you lie to me, my brother here is going to take a body part. Okay?"

Henry's eyes widen in terror and Conor pulls his head back further to emphasize that he is ready and waiting for my command. "Yes," he finally says.

"Why did you tell my brother that someone was looking for him?"

"Because this girl named Jessie asked me to, man. She seemed like she'd been crying and everything. She looked really upset," he babbles as he looks frantically around the room.

"If you're looking for help, there is none," I tell him. "The only way out of here is to help me find the people responsible for taking my brother."

"Okay, man. I'll help you. I'll do anything," he cries.

"How did you know who Mikey was?"

"She described him. Told me he was a big, good looking guy in a really expensive suit and with a beard. She said she really needed him and she was in trouble."

"What kind of trouble?"

"I don't know. I didn't ask. She was shaking, and she looked really scared and upset, man. Said she needed me to tell this Mikey guy that Jessie needed him and to come get her. That is all I know. I swear."

I sigh deeply before I nod to Conor and he grabs hold of one of Henry's earrings and rips it from his ear, making him cry out in pain.

"Next it will be your whole ear," I snarl as I step toward him, pushing my face closer to his. "Do you think we're playing here, kid?"

"No," he cries as he shakes his head. "But I don't know anything. I was just standing by the dance floor. My girl got us these VIP tickets, and I didn't want to waste them even after she went home. Then this chick just came up to me. She looked upset, like she'd been crying. She said she needed help and asked if I could go find Mikey for her. I swear that's all I know. I have no fucking clue who she was, man."

I glare at him. He is fucking trembling. His eyes are wide, his pupils dilated. He's sweating through his clothes. He blinks away a trickle of blood from his eye.

"He doesn't fucking know anything," I say with a sigh as I stand upright.

"I agree," Conor sighs too and lets Henry's head drop. "What now? Because we need to get rid of him."

"Hmm," I rub my jaw.

"What?" Henry shrieks. "I haven't done anything. I won't tell anyone anything. I swear."

"What is there to tell, Henry? You came to our club. You acted like a complete jackass and got thrown out by our bouncers and got that nasty cut on your eye in the process, right?"

He stares at me for a few seconds until the penny drops, and then he looks at me like I have just handed him a winning lottery ticket. "Yeah. Of course that's what happened," he nods furiously.

"I know where you live, Henry," I warn him. "I will find out where your girlfriend lives too."

He nods again. "I was a jackass. I got thrown out."

"You sure about this?" Conor arches an eyebrow at me and I signal to him that we should leave the room. "Drive the kid home and make sure you escort him inside. I want his address," I say to Chester once we're outside before I turn back to Conor. "We don't have time for this. The last thing I need to be doing tonight is disposing of a fucking body. And he's just a kid, Con."

"Yeah, but it would have felt good, Shane." He sucks in a breath and I wrap an arm around his shoulder.

"Yeah, it would. But we'll find him. Promise."

"Yeah. Of course we will."

"Let's go have a quick word with the rest of the bouncers and see if we get any more information that might be useful before we go see what Jessie and Mikey have come up with."

Conor nods his agreement and together we walk through the basement to the club.

CHAPTER
THREE

LIAM

My shoulder throbs like it's been speared by a red hot poker as I lie on the dusty floor of the van. I've got some kind of hood over my head, and my ankles and wrists are bound, but I listen to everything. I'm sure we've left the city and are on the freeway, but I have no idea where these pricks are taking me. They have been talking non fucking stop in Russian, making me regret not asking Jessie to teach me some when I had the chance so I could understand a single fucking word of what they're saying.

I shift my position to a more comfortable one, and someone kicks my ankles and mumbles something unintelligible.

"Fucking asshole," I shout as I kick both of my legs back at whoever it was, but all I hit is air and the sound of laughter fills the van, followed by more Russian voices. There are at least four of them in here with me. I feel so fucking stupid getting ambushed like that.

What the fuck! I should have been more vigilant. We knew they were going to attack sooner or later, and I let my guard down. I was so fucking relieved to have those two drunken college girls off my hands that I took my eye off the ball. And now I'm in the back of some disgusting van that, for some reason, stinks of fucking sausages and bacon grease and it makes me want to vomit into the bag on my head.

Fuck! I hope someone saw something, and my brothers are already on their way. But what if nobody saw anything? What if these fuckers are going to shoot me in the head, dump me in some ditch somewhere before anyone even notices that I'm missing? What if I never see my brothers or Jessie again?

My heart races in my chest so fast that I feel like it's going to burst through my ribcage. I try to take deep breaths, but the heavy cloth bag over my head doesn't exactly make that easy and I start to hyperventilate as I struggle to get enough air into my lungs.

Fuck! I can't breathe. I'm going to suffocate on the floor of this stinking, shit-box van. I can't die like this. Not here.

Think, Liam! Stop fucking freaking out like a scared little kid and think! What did Dr. Lisa used to tell Conor to do when he was having a panic attack or a nightmare?

The window. Yeah, that was it. Draw a window in your mind and follow the lines.

Breathe in for two.

Hold.

Out for two.

Hold.

And repeat.

As my breathing rate slows, I get more air into my lungs and my heart starts to calm down too. They will notice I've gone. They'll be looking for me right now. And they will come get me and take me home. And if they don't, I will haunt them for the rest of their goddamn lives.

FOUR

"Coffee, Red?" Mikey asks as he looks up at me from the laptop screen.

"Yes, please, I would love one," I say as I rub my eyes. We have been staring at these damn screens for a solid two hours. As I suspected, whoever tampered with the security feed has wiped some of the other cameras too. Specifically, the camera in the alleyway, where Conor met his mystery lady, has ten minutes missing so there is no evidence of her. And when we checked the camera for the main entrance, the footage of her talking to one of the bouncers from earlier had been wiped too, making it much harder to track her.

Sure enough, when Mikey checked the VIP area, there was no footage to be found of the woman claiming to be me approaching the guy with the green hair either, and a full ten minutes had been wiped. It doesn't mean that we can't find and track these people, it just makes it a hell of a lot harder.

But what is worrying me most is that I am systematically working my way through every security camera along this street and every single one has been hacked, and each of them has had a crucial portion of time wiped so that I have been unable to get eyes on the van that Liam was taken in. Which not only means that we are dealing with someone who really knows their shit, but it could take me days to find him, and we don't have that long.

"I'll be back in five then," Mikey says as he stands up and I smile at him because I can't let him see how worried I am.

I'm still bent over the screen when I hear someone walking into the room a moment later. "That was quick," I say without looking up.

"He didn't know anything useful," Conor replies and I look up to see him and Shane walking toward me.

"Really? Nothing at all?" I frown.

"No. You come up with anything yet?" Shane asks as he perches on the desk beside me.

I shake my head. "Nothing except that we are dealing with someone who knows their stuff."

I briefly explain the problems I've been encountering and watch as the worry and concern settle over Shane and Conor's faces.

"You can find him, though, Jessie?" Conor asks when I'm done.

"Yes. Of course I will." I glance at the computer screen. Liam has now been gone for almost three hours and who the hell knows what they are doing to him. "But I had hoped I'd have something by now. At the very least, I'd have wanted to identify the van that they took him in."

Conor sits on the sofa with his head in his hands while Shane nods solemnly. "What can we do to help?"

"Nothing right now," I admit. "All of these screens have something going on. I've got alerts set up for different traffic cameras. I have two programs trying to trace the IP address of whoever hacked the security footage, but none of those things are quick fixes."

Shane nods. "Maybe we need to find these college kids and this mystery woman who claimed she had Conor's baby?" he says.

"Conor's baby?" I stare at him open-mouthed.

"It wasn't. We'll explain later," Shane says with a sigh just as Mikey walks back into the office with a tray and a coffee for each of us.

"I heard you two coming back up," he says to Shane and Conor as he sets the tray down and hands each of us a drink. "You get anything from the kid with green hair?"

"No," Shane shakes his head. "Seems like he was just some random that they chose to deliver a message."

I lean back in my chair and blow on my hot coffee. "Not entirely random, though?" I arch an eyebrow at them as Mikey sits next to Conor.

"What do you mean?" Shane frowns.

"He had a green Mohawk, right?"

"Yeah," Mikey replies.

"How many guys do you see walking around your club, or even New York, with a hairstyle like that?"

"Not many," Mikey agrees.

"Are you suggesting we're not capable of getting information from people, Jessie?" Shane scowls at me.

"No," I shake my head. "Not at all. I'm sure he had none to offer and really was just a messenger. But why choose a guy with a green Mohawk? Why not pick someone who looks... well, average? Someone who doesn't stand out in a crowd?"

"You think they wanted us to be able to find him easily once we realized what had happened?" Shane asks.

"Yes. Exactly that." I nod as I take a sip of my coffee. "So, that your efforts are wasted interrogating some kid who genuinely has no clue what has gone on instead of focusing on the people who do."

"Fuck!" Conor says as he runs a hand over his face.

"So, who did have a clue what was going on?" Shane asks.

"No idea." I glance over at Conor and Mikey. "All three of you were distracted by young, attractive women, right?"

"Not me, Red," Mikey winks, unable to resist using humor to mask his emotions now that he is able to function again. "Mine was a guy with green hair."

Conor nudges him in the ribs and rolls his eyes. "Yeah. So?"

"But the guy with the green hair was approached by a young woman too. One he described as hot, right? That's no coincidence either, is it? I suppose those women could have been in on it, or could have been selected at random and paid off? I mean, there is no shortage of hot young women at your club, is there?"

"That's not really much help, sweetheart." Shane arches an eyebrow at me.

"It is though. Because it's a pattern, isn't it? Patterns are important because they are formulaic. The devil is in the detail, Shane Ryan. Has no one ever told you that?"

He stares at me as though I'm talking Spanish. "That particular pattern might be important and it might not, but identifying things like that helps me process. You have your methods of information gathering and I have mine," I shrug.

"I feel kind of helpless sitting here doing nothing and just watching you work though," Shane says and Conor and Mikey nod their agreement.

"You are helping," I say as I go back to my screen and continue my search. "Mikey, can you go through the footage in the club and track the two drunk college girls? Take screenshots of people they have more than a minute of conversation with, and then we can look into each of them."

"Okay. But that could take ages, Red."

"I understand that. But how else are we going to find out who these people were working for?"

He nods and sits at the laptop.

"And what about us?" Conor asks.

"Help Mikey if you can, but I need those other laptops to keep doing their thing, so you'll have to look over his shoulder or find another one."

"There's one in the club downstairs," Conor says before walking out of the office.

"And me?" Shane asks.

"Keep talking. Tell me everything the guy with the green hair said."

Shane relays the information they got from the guy downstairs while I continue my painstaking search of all the traffic cameras in the New York district, starting with the ones closest to us and working outwards. I try to hide my frustration as each one has been tampered with in the same way. I have no idea how long this will go on for because the person tampering with them is constantly two steps ahead of me, and they are incredibly thorough. I will catch up with them eventually, but it could take vital time that we don't have. So, until my software tracks their IP address, I am screwed.

"Anything?" Conor asks when he comes back into the room fifteen minutes later, as I sit frowning at the computer screen.

"Not yet," I shake my head. Nothing from their conversation with the Mohawk guy has given me anything else to work with, so I go on with my search while the brothers check the CCTV from the club.

ANOTHER HOUR HAS PASSED and we are still no closer to finding Liam. The tension in the room is ratcheting up with each passing minute as the boys' frustration grows that they are unable to do something more to find their brother. My methods are definitely not what they are used to, but right now we have little else to go on.

"Any luck?" I pop my head over the computer and ask Mikey.

"No," he says with a sigh. "Nobody except Liam and one of the bouncers spoke to them for more than a few seconds."

"They could have been approached before they even got to the club?" Conor suggests.

"Yeah, or they were in on it from the outset," Mikey adds.

I nod absent-mindedly. "Or they were spoken to in a place where there are no cameras?"

"The ladies' room?" Shane frowns.

"Maybe." I shrug.

"Mikey, concentrate on the cameras outside the ladies' room. Look for the college girls and a hot redhead," Shane barks.

"On it," Mikey grins, no doubt believing that we are finally getting somewhere, although I'm not so sure. I can't shake the feeling that the young women were pawns, just like the green-haired guy, and are more dead end leads to keep us from following the right ones.

"Are we sure it was the Russians who took him?" Shane frowns as he rubs a hand over his jaw and looks at Conor. "Perhaps you and I should go and shake up a few of our associates and see what they know?"

"It had to be the Russians," Conor frowns at him. "No one else would pull shit like this. No one else has anything to gain from taking Liam."

"But why Liam? What do they have to gain from taking him?" Shane frowns.

I sit back in my chair. It is the most obvious question with the most obvious answer. The one we should have asked from the outset. Because I just realized exactly where they have taken him.

"Me," I say, and the three of them turn to stare at me. "Alexei wants me."

"Yeah," Conor frowns.

"So, that's the point of it all. Throw us into a tailspin, chasing leads that go nowhere until we finally realize that it is me he wants."

"But we already knew that, Angel," Conor says.

"We did. But we kind of forgot that in our search for Liam," I say as I bring up the traffic camera I am looking for. I do a quick calculation in my head to account for driving time and search a fifteen minute window either side. Thankfully, at 2:30am there is little traffic, and sure enough the black van appears on the screen in front of me.

"So, where the hell have they taken him?"

"To the house in Connecticut," I say as I nod toward the screen. "He wanted us to find him. He knew we would come for him, and that is the surest way to get me back."

Shane leans down and wraps his arm around me, pressing a kiss on the top of my head. "Good girl," he says softly before he stands upright again.

"Mikey, grab every fucking explosive device you can get your hands on. Conor, get the guns. The big ones." Shane barks his orders.

"Jessie. Go get dressed, sweetheart. Because we are about to go and bury Alexei Ivanov and his Bratva army."

I nod and stand up from my chair, grateful that he didn't try to make me sit this out, because there is not a chance in hell I would have.

"Meet in the basement in twenty," Shane shouts to his brothers' retreating backs as they march out of the room.

CHAPTER
FIVE
JESSIE

I shift my weight from foot to foot as we wait for Conor and Mikey. I came down to the basement five minutes ago and Shane was down here already. He has started up the giant armored SUV and has left the engine running while we wait for his brothers.

"You don't have to come with us, Jessie. You can stay here where it's safe. I'll have my best men here watching you," he offers.

"Are you kidding me, Shane?" I frown at him. "He has Liam. Because of me. Alexei is responsible for killing my whole family. He lied to me. Drugged me. Manipulated me into believing that you were the enemy. I want to look into his eyes while he takes his last breath." I spit the final words as the venom I feel for him spills out of me.

"Okay." Shane narrows his eyes at me.

"You think I won't be able to do it, don't you?"

"I never said that," he shakes his head.

"No. You don't have to. I can see it. You think I don't have the guts to follow it through."

"You have bigger balls that almost every man I've ever

known, sweetheart. I have no doubt you could do it. But do you want to live with that?"

"I've lived with much worse these past ten years."

He nods and steps closer toward me, with his hands in his trouser pockets. "Let me do this for you, Jessie."

"Why? Do you think I'm weak?"

"Weak? No. You are titanium. But I would die if anything happened to you."

"Shane!" I breathe.

"Or my brothers," he adds quickly. "I should have killed our father. For everything he did to me and my brothers. For what he did to our mom. I had the perfect opportunity to. I pressed the gun against his forehead and he just stared up at me, slobbering and crying because he was steaming drunk. And I couldn't do it. And I've fucking hated myself for it ever since. I don't want you to have to live with any regrets. Let me kill him for you and you won't have to."

"I'm sorry that you've lived with that, Shane. I don't know what happened to you all. Conor told me some of what he went through. I do know that your brothers wouldn't have survived their childhoods without you. But I can't let you kill Alexei for me. I still have so many questions left to ask him. I need to look him in the eyes and ask him why."

"What if he doesn't give you the answers you're looking for, Jessie?"

"Then I'll have to find the Wolf and ask him instead."

Shane smiles at me. "Just know that I'll be one step behind you all the way, Hacker. Okay?"

"Thank you," I smile too. "I appreciate you having my back."

"I'll always have your back, sweetheart," he says and there is a moment of connection between us that almost takes my breath away.

"We ready to go?" Mikey shouts from behind us and I turn

to see him and Conor striding through the basement, looking like they are about to go to war, and I suppose that we are.

"Yes. Let's go," Shane nods and the four of us climb into the car. Shane and Conor in the front, and Mikey and me in the back. The shutters are open and Shane guns the engine and speeds out of the basement garage. Mikey stares out the window in silence and Conor leans his head back against the headrest. I reach through and put my hand on Conor's shoulder and squeeze, and he places his warm, strong hand over mine. I reach for Mikey's hand with my other one and he takes it, curling his fingers around mine as Shane goes over the plan, which is basically to plow through the gates, blow everything up and find Liam as quickly as possible while killing as many Russians as we can.

"We'll have him home in a few hours," he says confidently and we all nod our agreement. I swallow hard as I lean back and stare out the window. My hand is still wrapped in Mikey's and he holds it tightly. The atmosphere in the car is thick with tension and I know that we are all probably thinking about the same thing. What lengths will Alexei go to in order to ensure I come back to him? What is he doing to Liam right now, and will we get our boy back alive?

CHAPTER

SIX

MIKEY

As I stare out the window, my heart races faster as we get closer to Alexei's Connecticut fortress. I try to concentrate on the sensation of Jessie's warm, soft fingers holding onto mine. Images of Alexei and his men torturing my twin force themselves into my brain and I have to force them back out. I need to stay focused, because I can't let Liam down. *We* can't let him down. Because I have no idea how I'll even keep breathing if we don't get him out of there and home to us. I don't know how any of us would get over it. Even Jessie. She has only been a part of our family for a short time, but she is inextricably linked to us now, and I know she feels the pain of Alexei taking him as deeply as we do.

It was a sight to behold to see her working earlier, and in different circumstances, I would have been content to sit and watch her do her thing for hours, because she is a fucking genius. But I could hardly focus on anything except getting Liam back. I probably hindered her more than I helped her, with my constant questions and my pacing, but if I did, she never gave me any indication of that fact.

Now it's my turn to step up. Because blowing shit up,

killing, and maiming is my thing, and I will go through anyone I need to in order to make sure I get my twin and the rest of us out of there safely.

"We're almost there, Mikey," Conor says as he turns in his seat. "What you got for us?" He nods to the huge black duffle bag at my feet.

"Bombs. Lots of bombs. And some tear gas," I reply.

"Tear gas?" Shane asks.

"Yep. But I got us some masks," I reach down and unzip the bag before pulling out the four gas masks.

"Nice," Conor says with a nod as I pass two into the front for him and Shane. Jessie stares down at hers as I pass her one too.

"You ever worn one of these, Red?" I ask her.

She shakes her head.

I tighten the strap for her. "Put it on when I tell you to, and don't take it off until you see us do the same. Or you're completely clear of the hallway. Okay?"

"Okay," she nods.

"Pass me the bag from the back, bro," Conor says and I reach behind the seat and pull out his bag of tricks before handing them to him.

"Any preferences?" he asks as opens up the zip.

"Semi-automatic and a Beretta for me," I reply.

"Same," Shane adds.

"And what about you, Angel?" Conor turns to her and smiles.

"I've never used a semi-automatic before, but I'm game if you have a spare. And I'll take a Beretta too."

Conor pokes his head into the bag. "Will a Glock do?"

"Sure. As long as it will take out Alexei Ivanov, I'm easy," she shrugs.

I feel the tension in the car growing at the mention of his name. We all want Alexei.

24

"I won't let you down. Promise," she says as she looks between the three of us.

"We know." I squeeze her hand.

Conor and Shane nod their agreement. It is only fair that Jessie is given the chance to ice her father after everything he did to her and her family.

"But if one of us gets a clean shot..." Shane adds, not needing to finish the sentence.

"I understand," she says quietly.

"You clear on the plan?" Shane says as we approach the mansion where Liam is being held.

"Yeah," the rest of us reply.

The plan is simple enough. We drive through the gates and right through the front doors of the house in this car, which is basically an armored tank. Then comes the tear gas, the bombs and the shooting. Kill anything that moves that isn't one of us. Spread out and find our boy.

CHAPTER
SEVEN
JESSIE

The entire ground floor of Alexei's mansion is carnage. They were prepared for us, but I don't think they expected us so soon. It seems like Mikey has blown up half the house, and the explosions, along with the tear gas, have taken out the first wave of Alexei's men. The gas masks prevent us inhaling the smoke from the bombs too and we are able to move freely through the haze. Mikey indicates his head that he's heading toward the kitchen and Conor heads upstairs. I remember my father and Vlad referring to holding rooms in the basement when I was here.

I tap Shane on the shoulder. "I think he might be downstairs."

Before he can reply, half a dozen of Alexei's men appear out of nowhere, coming in through the hole in the wall that was the front entrance only a few minutes earlier. They run toward us and we dive for cover behind the marble staircase.

"Go. I'll meet you down there," Shane shouts as he jumps up and takes two of them out. They fire back and I contemplate staying and helping.

"Go, Hacker!" he orders. I hand him my semi-automatic so

he has two and can hold off these guys more easily before I make a run for the basement stairwell, pulling the Glock from my waistband as I do.

As I reach the bottom of the stairwell, two men run toward me. I squeeze out two quick rounds and they drop to the floor. I hate guns, but I have been using them since I was eighteen and I have a perfect aim. Pulling off my mask, I toss it onto the floor. There is no smoke or tear gas down here.

I edge along the quiet hallway, praying that Liam is down here and he is still alive. As I approach the first room, I steel myself to look inside. When I do, it's empty and my heart rate increases as I approach the second one. When I find that empty too, I glance toward the end of the hallway to the room at the back. If Liam is down here, he must be in there. As I make my way closer, the adrenaline starts to thunder around my body and I take a deep breath to calm my breathing and my racing heart. I need to stay calm and prepare myself for whatever I may, or may not, find in that room. Because if Liam and Alexei are in there, then this might be my only chance.

I draw level with the room, and unlike the others, the door is closed. My fingers grip the handle and I take a beat. *You got this, Jessie.*

As I push open the door, a man is standing directly in front of me, with his hand raised and the barrel of a gun aimed at my head. He doesn't have time to squeeze the trigger before I put a bullet in his neck. He drops to the floor and the sight behind him almost stops my heart. Alexei has Liam chained to the floor. Jumper cables and bloodied instruments lie scattered on the ground around them and the entire room is filled with the metallic smell of blood, making me wonder how much of Liam's has been spilled in here.

I watch my father holding up Liam's battered and broken body by his hair, and my throat constricts as I struggle to take in air. They've had him for a little over six hours and yet have inflicted so much damage. I resist the urge to run to him and wrench him from my father's cruel grasp. Above me, the sound of gunshots and carnage can be heard as the rest of the Ryan brothers tear this house and its occupants to pieces.

At least I hope that's what is happening. But the reality of our situation is slowly starting to sink in. Alexei's army outnumbers us by at least five to one. He could have called for reinforcements by now. I could lose one, or even all of them here today, and that thought makes me feel like my heart has been torn from my chest.

"You came home, printsessa," Alexei sneers. "I knew that you would."

I raise the Glock in my hand and aim at his face. He laughs at me and shakes his head. "You won't use that."

"Try me, *Papa*. Now let him go."

"You couldn't kill me to save your own life, Jessica. You think I believe you'll kill me to save his?" he snarls as he jerks Liam's head and causes him to groan in pain. The sound slices a welt across my heart.

"Please let him go, Papa!"

He narrows his eyes at me. "Have you learned nothing from me, printsessa? What makes you think I will allow any of these Irish pigs to live even one more day after they stole you from me?"

I glance at Liam and my heart begins to break into a million pieces. The sound of an explosion above us makes me and my father look up and he starts to laugh again. "My men will be making sure your friends pay for their crimes. While you stand here pretending you have the balls to kill me."

My pulse is thrumming against my skin as my blood thunders around my body. What if Shane and Conor and Mikey are hurt too? How the hell do I get us all out of this alive? I have one last bargaining chip at my disposal — me. "Let him go and I'll come home, Papa. If it's me you want, then I'm yours."

"But you're already mine, Jessica," he frowns at me.

"You don't understand." I shake my head. "I'll stay. Of my own free will. I will try and be the daughter that you want me to be, Papa. I will marry whoever you choose for me. I will give you grandbabies. But only if you let my friends go."

"You'd do that for him?" he sneers as he jerks Liam's head again.

"Yes."

"Why?" he spits.

"Because if you kill him, you will destroy me. If you kill any of them, you will destroy everything I have left. You took one family from me, Papa. Please don't take them too. I promise I will try to be a good daughter for you, but please give me something. Show me that there is something in you worth trying to love," I plead with him. I see his eyes soften at the corners and the hint of a smile plays on his lips. For a second I wonder if he is considering my proposal, but his smile turns cruel and mocking.

"I murdered my own brother and the only woman I have ever loved, printsessa. Alexei Ivanov is not a man of mercy," he sneers as he raises his arm and I see the glint of a blade as he brings it toward Liam's neck. Before he can make contact, I squeeze the trigger of my gun and the blade clatters to the floor as Alexei clutches his throat where the bullet has just torn straight through it. He drops to the floor and I run to Liam, catching him before he hits the ground too.

"Liam." I smooth the blood matted hair from his forehead. "I'm here, baby. I've got you," I say as I wrap him in my arms. The sound of Alexei choking on his own blood next to us is of little comfort as I wonder at the easiest way to get Liam out of this place and to a hospital as quickly as possible. He can't stand and there is no way I can lift him. But like an answer to my prayers, Shane is right beside me.

"You did good, Hacker. Now let's get him out of here," he says as he hoists Liam up and onto his shoulder.

"How long have you been in here?" I pant with the effort of lifting Liam's weight.

"Long enough. Now let's go. We need to get him to the car."

As we're making our way out of the room, I steal a quick glance back at Alexei. His blood pools on the floor beneath him as he lies there with lifeless eyes. But I can't take a chance. Too many ghosts from my past haunt me. I won't allow another one to do that. I raise my gun again and discharge my remaining bullets into his motionless body.

Shane stands with Liam and waits for me. When I'm done, I take half of Liam's weight again and we leave the room without another word. We meet up with Conor and Mikey along the hallway and I'm relieved to see they are both unharmed. They both run to us, but it is Mikey who takes his twin from me and Shane, lifting his brother into his arms.

"The car is still out front. We need to check him over and see if we need to head to the ER," Shane snaps as he indicates the door.

"Then let's get the fuck out of here," Conor snarls as we turn for the exit.

Before we reach it, my father's second in command, Vlad, steps into our path out of nowhere.

Shane points a gun at Vlad's head, and the Russian holds his hands out in surrender as his eyes lock on me. "Where are you going? This is all yours now, Jessica," he says as he looks around the huge mansion.

"What? Are you serious?"

"You're the only surviving member of the Ivanov family," he says solemnly. "You are the new head of the Bratva."

Shane and Conor stare at me while Mikey shifts Liam's weight in his arms.

"I am *not* the head of the Bratva!" I snarl.

"But, this is all yours."

"You can have it, Vlad. I don't want any of it. You were his second, so you take over." I spent more time with Vlad than I did Alexei the last time I was at this mansion, after my father lured me here under false pretenses. My instincts tell me he is a better man than his predecessor ever was.

"I don't understand," he frowns at me.

"I hate the Bratva. They've taken everything from me."

"But, you are Jessica Ivanov. You *are* the Bratva," he replies, as though he's unable to comprehend why I wouldn't want this.

"Jessica Ivanov died ten years ago. My name is Jessie Ryan."

Conor takes hold of my hand and squeezes and moves to stand beside me.

Vlad stares at me for a few seconds, and then he nods his head in comprehension.

"I trust there will be no more bloodshed between our families?" I say to him.

"Of course not. It is done. I wish you a long and happy life, Jessie Ryan," he says as he steps aside and allows us all to walk freely past him.

EIGHT

S itting on the back seat of the SUV, I cradle Liam's head on my lap as he drifts in and out of consciousness. Conor drives as fast as the car will allow, while Shane talks on the phone, making arrangements for their personal physician, Dr. Lisa Adams, and a surgeon friend of hers to be waiting at the apartment for us as soon as we get back. Shane and Conor quickly checked Liam over as soon as we got him to the car and decided we should head straight home.

Mikey sits in the back seat with Liam and me, staring anxiously at his injured twin brother.

"Are you sure we shouldn't take him straight to the hospital?" I ask when Shane ends his call to Lisa.

"No!" the three of them answer in unison.

"He will freak the fuck out if he wakes up in hospital, Red," Mikey says. "He's fucking terrified of those places. We both are."

"Lisa and Matt will have everything we need at the apartment," Shane adds. "This isn't the first time we've dealt with something like this, Jessie," Shane growls from the front seat.

"Okay," I reply as tears prick at my eyes. Liam is lying here bleeding on my lap, and if he doesn't make it, I have no idea what we will do. There is so much emotion and tension in this car, I can't wait to get out of it and into the apartment. I will feel a million times better when Liam is in the hands of Lisa and the surgeon.

"No hospitals," Liam mumbles as his eyelids flicker open.

I look down at his beautiful face and place my hand on his cheek. "Of course not," I smile at him.

He smiles back as his eyelids flutter closed again. "I heard what you said, Jessie."

I suck in a deep breath. I said a lot of things in that room.

"You were going to stay with him. For me?" he mumbles the words.

"Shush now. You need to save your energy," I tell him as I lean down and softly kiss his forehead, but an unexpected tear falls from my eyes and onto his face. I brush it away gently with the pads of my fingertips.

"Don't cry, baby. I hate it when you cry. And I'm the happiest man in the world right now," he smiles before he drifts back into unconsciousness.

I look up and Mikey is staring at me now with tears in his eyes.

"He'll be okay," I say with a confidence I don't fully trust in.

Mikey nods. "You were going to stay with Alexei?" he frowns at me.

I swallow hard. "It was the heat of the moment. I had no idea what was happening upstairs. He had a knife to Liam's throat." I choke back the tears. "I told him I would stay if he would guarantee that the four of you walked out of there alive." I wipe another tear as it rolls down my cheek.

I realize that Shane will have already heard me say some of that stuff because he was standing in the doorway of that room, and now Conor keeps glancing at me in the rearview mirror too.

"Even if it meant leaving us and living with a man you despise?" Mikey asks.

"I would do anything for you," I whisper. "Isn't that what being a family is? Wouldn't you sacrifice yourself for your brothers if you believed you had no choice?"

Mikey stares at me, and I feel Conor's eyes on me through the mirror. "You can be pissed at me all you want, but I would do it again in a heartbeat," I sniff.

Mikey reaches out his hand and takes mine in his, squeezing gently. "I'm not pissed at you, Red. I think you're a fucking queen. You just turned down the Bratva empire and shot your own father for us. I'm fucking honored to call you mine." He lifts my hand to his lips and kisses it softly. "But know there is not a chance in hell that we would have left that place without you."

He leans back in his seat and closes his eyes with my hand still clasped in his. I can't see Shane's face because he is sitting directly in front of me, but I see the hint of a smile on Conor's lips as he keeps his eyes fixed on the road ahead, driving us all back to safety.

CHAPTER
NINE

SHANE

L isa and her surgeon boyfriend, Matt, were waiting for us as soon as we got back to the apartment, with their equipment set up in Liam and Mikey's room. Liam was still drifting in and out of consciousness, but I trust that I am placing him in the best possible hands. My baby brother is one of the toughest men I've ever known. I suspect he's concussed and lost a lot of blood, but I won't be able to breathe again until Lisa tells me that he's going to be okay. They are in the room with him now, while Jessie, my brothers and I wait anxiously in the hallway.

Jessie chews her nails. Mikey paces up and down muttering to himself. Conor leans against the wall with his eyes closed and I do a combination of all of that because the waiting is fucking killing me.

"Should we just fucking go in and see what's going on?" Mikey eventually snaps.

I glance at my watch. "They've only been in there with him for twenty minutes, Mikey. Let them do their thing. Lisa knows how worried we are. She'll come out here and tell us what's going on as soon as she can."

He takes a deep breath, his brow furrowed in frustration and worry. "Fine," he snaps and goes to stand next to Jessie, who stops chewing her nails and wraps her arms around his neck instead. He drops his head low, resting it against her shoulder while she rubs his back with one hand and runs the other one through his hair. It seems to calm him down because he stands still.

I stand still too, watching her with him. I heard everything she said to Alexei earlier today. She would never have had to go through with it because I was ready to drop him as soon as he made a move, only she had the balls to do it herself anyway. I'm still not sure if I'm pissed or impressed that she was willing to do that for us. The fact that she would give up her life and spend it with him to save the four of us, should make me proud of her. It should show me that she truly is one of us, willing to sacrifice her own happiness for ours. I would do the same for my brothers, and for her too, and I know that they would do the same for me. But she still doesn't get that there is no happiness for any of them without her. I wonder if there is any for me without her either.

It's been forty minutes since Lisa closed that door and left us out here so she and Matt could treat Liam. It has seemed like an eternity and the tension in this hallway is so thick that I could slice through it. When I wonder how much more of this we can all stand, the door opens and Mikey runs toward it. Lisa has one of those faces that is unreadable. I'm sure it's a skill she has honed over the years having to give families and loved ones difficult news, but it means she also has that same damn expression when she is giving good news too. And for a few seconds, my whole world stops turning.

"He's going to be okay," she says and only then does she

smile as Mikey picks her up and almost squeezes the life from her. My heart starts to beat again and the relief courses through me.

"Thank fuck, doc!" Conor shouts as he walks over to Lisa, pulling her into another bear hug as soon as Mikey puts her down. Jessie hovers behind them with a huge smile on her face and tears in her eyes and I instinctively reach out to her and pull her toward me. I have no doubt that she has been blaming herself for Liam being taken by Alexei, and I also know that she is just as happy as we are to find out that he is going to be okay.

I wrap my arms around her and she melts into me, pressing her face against my chest as she starts to cry quietly while the tension and the fear she's been carrying for the past twelve hours slips away from her. I hold her there as the sobs convulse through her body, allowing her to let it all go so that she can be strong again when she sees him.

"You did good, Hacker," I say as I press a soft kiss on the top of her head and regret it because I smell her hair and it reminds me of all of the other times I have kissed her. My pulse quickens, and the blood rushes south as though my entire body is hardwired to want her.

"You can go in and see him now," Lisa says and Jessie stands straight, wiping the tears from her face with the sleeve of her hooded sweatshirt. "I've given him some strong pain relief and it will be kicking in very soon, so you only have a few minutes before he's out."

"Let's get in there," I say, and Jessie and my brothers walk into the room in front of me.

"Thanks, doc," I say to Lisa as I reach her, wrapping an arm around her shoulders.

"You're welcome. Go see him, and I'll bring you up to speed on the damage and his aftercare in a few minutes."

Walking into the room, I see Liam lying in bed, covered in

dressings and bandages and dried blood, and even though he is groggy, he is awake. Jessie and my brothers crowd around him and he smiles at them all. "I told you I'd be fine. Doc says I'm invincible," he mumbles and Mikey and Conor start to tease him about only wanting time off work, while Jessie gives him a kiss on the cheek. He reaches for her and wraps his bandaged hand around her fingers. "Come in here with me, baby," he attempts a wink but the meds are kicking in and he doesn't quite manage it.

"Maybe later, sunshine," she laughs and he smiles goofily at her.

I walk around to where she is standing, and she tries to move aside to let me in, but he refuses to let go of her hand. "Come here, big bro," Liam insists as he waves me toward him with his other hand, so I have to squeeze in behind her until my body is pressed against her ass. Please do not let my cock get hard right now!

I reach my arm over Jessie's shoulder and put my hand on his hair, which is still matted with blood. "Get some sleep, kid."

"So fucking bossy," he slurs his words as his eyelids close and I am able to step back and away from Jessie with a sigh of relief.

AFTER LIAM FALLS into his drug induced sleep, Jessie and Mikey stay in his room while Matt does some final checks and Lisa, Conor and I walk to my office.

"So, what's the damage?" I ask when we are all seated.

"Fortunately, it is mostly superficial. He has three broken ribs, and they will hurt, but they will heal with rest. His shoulder and knee were both dislocated, but I have reset them. He has a couple of broken fingers on his left hand, which we've bandaged up. We've stitched his lacerations. Treated his burns, which shouldn't scar badly, except, perhaps, for one on his back. He had one of his molars and one of his wisdom teeth ripped out, but that shouldn't cause him any ongoing issues. He has no internal bleeding that we can detect and nothing that will require any further treatment. Except his dressings will need to be changed regularly. He was smiling when I told him that because he said that Jessie is going to be his nurse." She arches an eyebrow at us and I can't help laughing.

"I bet he was," Conor laughs too.

"Overall, he is just pretty beat up and he is going to need lots of rest to allow his body to heal. He's experienced significant trauma, and if he tries to push himself too soon, his recovery will take much longer. You need to make sure he takes it easy," she warns us both.

"We will," I say with a nod.

"And he also has a concussion," she adds. "Who knows how long that could take to heal. It could be days. It could be months. But just keep an eye on him, and like I said, make sure he gets plenty of rest."

"Yeah. Rest," Conor nods. "We will."

"I mean proper rest. Like bed rest." She arches an eyebrow at Conor because after we rescued him from the Russians two years ago, he refused to rest for longer than an hour at a time.

"We'll make sure he does," I assure her.

"Yeah. And trust me, doc, I would have stayed on bed rest too if I'd had the nurse that Liam is going to have." Conor flashes his eyebrows at us both and Lisa laughs.

"Yes. I noticed Jessie is back. For good this time?" she asks.

"Yes. For good," Conor answers her before I even have a chance to open my mouth. But I nod my agreement when Lisa looks my way.

"Great. I'm going to get back in there and help Matt get cleaned up, and I'll talk to Jessie and Mikey about how to change his dressings. I also noticed Jessie has a cut on her cheek which I want to have a look at. Are either of you hurt?" she glances between the two of us.

"No," we both reply in unison.

"Okay. I'll leave you both to it then," she says as she stands.

"Thanks again, Lisa," I tell her before she leaves the room.

"Anytime," she says, but she has a serious expression on her face. "But I wish you boys would retire. Because I am terrified that one of these days I'm going to be discussing taking a body to the morgue instead of trying to enforce bed rest."

I suck in a deep breath as I watch her walk out of the room.

"Well, that was sobering," Conor says with a grin.

"She'll kick your ass if she sees you grinning like that," I warn him as I smile at him too. Lisa is right, and we both know it, but right now we are too fucking relieved that our baby brother is okay to be anything other than thrilled.

"You want to come bring the guns up from the car while Lisa and Matt finish up?" I suggest, wanting something useful to do.

"Why not?" he agrees with a smile and we walk out of my office together.

It doesn't take Conor and me very long to clear the car of weapons, and we leave them in one of our safe rooms in the basement before heading back upstairs. We talked the whole time we worked, about the club, about the football, about the new bar staff our manager hired, all the while avoiding the elephant in the room that is me and Jessie.

As we stand in the elevator on our way back to the penthouse, I feel Conor's eyes burning into me.

"What is it?"

He turns his body toward me. "You know that I respect the hell out of you, right?"

"Yeah."

"And you are the person I trust most in this whole world?"

"Yeah. So?"

"So, understand that I say this with the greatest of respect and love for you as my brother, and the man who raised me, but you are a fucking fool."

"What?" I blink at him. After the start of that speech, I had no idea this is where it would go.

"What the hell does she have to do to prove herself to you, Shane? She gave up everything for us and that's still not enough for you?"

"It doesn't change anything, Conor," I snap.

"Really?" he shakes his head at me.

"Really."

"You have this incredible, strong, kind, sexy woman who fucking adores you and you're letting her slip away from you because of some stupid rule you have about not giving people second chances. And I know that you love her too, Shane. I see the way you can't take your fucking eyes off her. So, if you want to die on this *you only get one chance with me* hill, then be my guest. It's one less person I have to share her with," he says as the doors open and he walks out, leaving me to stare after him, wondering if he has a point.

TEN

JESSIE

I walk out of Liam's bedroom and lean back against the wall, letting the waves of relief wash over me. Lisa and Matt have checked Liam's dressing again and all of the bleeding has stopped. His injuries are all going to heal. There will be no permanent damage. He is going to be okay. Alexei is dead. We're all safe.

The door opens again and Shane steps out of the room. He stands directly in front of me and I swallow as I stare at him.

He reaches out and brushes his hand over the cut on my cheek, his fingertips leaving trails of electricity in their wake. "Did you get that looked at?" he frowns, his face full of concern.

"Yes," I rub my own fingers over it absent-mindedly. "Lisa insisted on looking at it. It doesn't need stitches and there is no fracture."

"Good," he whispers.

"You okay?" I look him over and don't see any obvious injuries.

"Yeah. Now that we know Liam is okay," he nods and I see his Adam's apple bob. Why does he look so damn nervous? Holy fuck! Just when I thought I was going to have some time to take a breath, Shane is about to hit me with another bombshell. I can sense it. Is he going to ask me to leave now that we've dealt with Alexei?

"I should get back in there to him," I say, but he puts a hand beside my head on the wall and stops me from moving. I stare at him, and the change in his face is almost instantaneous. There is no nervous energy there now.

"No," he shakes his head. "He's going to be knocked out for the rest of the day and night. I've asked Conor and Mikey to stay with him."

"But I want to stay too," I protest. Why isn't he letting me back into the room?

"I get that. And I know he'll need you when he wakes up, but that won't be for at least eighteen hours. The doc has given him some heavy duty shit."

"So? In the meantime, I do what?"

He takes a step closer to me as he places his other hand on the wall beside me until I am caged in by him. My breath catches in my throat as the heat from his body penetrates the thin fabric of my tank top, and I unconsciously bite my lip.

"Dammit, Jessie," he groans. "Do you have any idea what you do to me?"

"Push your buttons?" I arch an eyebrow at him, trying to ease the growing tension from whatever the hell is going on here.

He edges closer, until our bodies are just a few inches apart. "Well, yeah. You drive me fucking crazy." He narrows his eyes at me.

"You didn't answer my question. What am I supposed to be doing if I can't stay with Liam?" I breathe, because the answer that is becoming increasingly more obvious, can't be the right one. He's made it more than clear we can be nothing more than friends.

He presses his body against mine until I'm pinned against the wall by him and the wet heat rushes between my thighs. "Liam will need you tomorrow and probably every night for the next week. But I need you now, sweetheart. Stay with me?"

I draw in a deep breath as pleasure floods my body and a whole raft of emotions overwhelm my senses. "Just tonight?"

"Well, I've thought about tying you to my bed and keeping you there forever, but I think my brothers would kill me. Besides, like I said, Liam will want you there when he wakes up tomorrow." He drops his head to my neck and plants soft kisses along my collarbone, and my legs tremble as the heat flushes across my chest.

"You're not playing fair," I pant as I writhe beneath his touch and he responds by pressing his body even closer to mine. His hard cock digs into my abdomen and I bite my lip as I try to stop myself from groaning his goddamn name. This man is a devil, and he plays my body like a finely tuned instrument.

"I never play fair, sweetheart," he murmurs against my skin as his kisses move up my neck, and the soft scratch of his stubble on the delicate skin sends pleasure skittering along my spine. "So, what's your answer, and I will warn you, there's only one I'll accept."

I plant my hands on his chest. I need to stop his maddening teasing because I can't think straight at all, but he grabs my wrists and pins them against the wall either side of my head and glares into my eyes, as though he is trying to peer inside my soul.

"Is that so?" I narrow my eyes at him.

"Yes."

"Then it isn't really a question, is it? More of a demand?"

"Semantics," he says with a shrug.

"You're an arrogant asshole, Shane Ryan," I try to scowl, but somehow I can only smile. "And I believe that I asked you a question too."

"And what was that?" he says as he starts his maddening teasing again, peppering soft kisses along my throat as he grinds his cock against my groin.

"Do you only want me for tonight? Is this a one time thing?"

He lifts my wrists above my head so he can pin them easily with one hand, while his free hand slides down to the button of my jeans. He opens it easily before he pulls down my zipper and slips his hand inside my panties and between my thighs and the rush of wet heat makes me gasp out loud. "Just say yes, Jessie?" he growls, while not answering my question at all.

"Shane," I groan loudly and he chuckles against my skin.

"Fuck! You're soaking wet. Are you ready to answer me yet, Hacker?" he growls.

"No," I breathe.

He doesn't seem fazed at all by my response. "No, you're not ready to answer, or no, you won't spend the night with me."

"No, I won't spend the night with you," I hiss as he begins to rub my clit in slow, teasing circles.

"Wrong answer, Jessie," he growls as his kisses become fiercer and he sucks on my neck as his hand slides further into my panties before he pushes a finger inside me.

"Shane!" I cry out as he begins to finger fuck me against the wall in the hallway. "What if Lisa or Matt come out here?" I breathe as my body shudders from the orgasm he's already coaxing from me.

"Then let me take you to bed and I'll fuck you properly," he groans as he keeps on thrusting his fingers in and out of me and rubbing the knuckle of his thumb over my clit. I hear voices approaching the doorway and swear one of them is female. Shit! Dr. Lisa is going to come out here and hear me come while

Shane finger bangs me, and I will die of embarrassment because I don't think anything is going to make him stop.

"Okay!" I finally relent.

"Good girl," he says with a deviant smile as he slides his hand from my panties. Then he looks me in the eye as he sucks his fingers clean and the wet heat floods my core. He releases my wrists and takes hold of one of my hands instead.

I stand there, looking at his face. Damn, I love him so much. My body is practically screaming for his touch. "Shane," I say as he is about to start walking us to his room.

He stops and turns back to me. "What is it?" he frowns.

"I can't do this with you," I shake my head, realizing this was a huge mistake. "I'm sorry. But I can't do that with you. Not anymore."

His Adam's apple bobs as he swallows hard. "Can't do what, Jessie?"

"Just sex," I whisper. "It would mean so much more to me than that. I can't just turn off my emotions like that, and I can't only have a part of you when I know what it's like to have all of you."

He steps back and pushes me against the wall, his hand fisting in my hair and his mouth crashing over mine. He kisses me so fiercely that my lips feel bruised and I whimper into his mouth. When I expect I might pass out from lack of oxygen and the raging endorphins racing around my body, he lets us up for air. "Just give me one night, Hacker?" he presses his forehead against mine. "I need you."

I take a deep breath and, despite every part of my body aching for him, I push him away. "I can't, Shane," I shake my head. "I'm not some toy you get to use when you have an itch to scratch. Not if I can't have all of you. I'm sorry."

"I can't give you all of me, Jessie," he breathes. "Not again."

"I understand that," I say as the tears sting my eyes.

"Can't this be enough?" he says, his eyes pleading with me and weakening my resolve with each passing second.

"No. And I know that it might be unfair, but I need all or nothing, Shane. Because you will always have all of me." I plant a soft kiss on his lips and then I walk back into Liam's room. I don't even dare glance at him again because I might run back into his arms and tell him that one night with him is worth the pain of losing him all over again.

CHAPTER
ELEVEN
CONOR

As Lisa and Matt are preparing to leave, the bedroom door opens and Jessie walks back inside the room, and I can't help but frown as she makes her way over to the chair beside the bed and sits down on it. It's a little after midday but none of us have slept for over twenty four hours and we all need some rest.

Ten minutes earlier, Shane asked me and Mikey to stay with Liam for the rest of the day and tonight, so I had assumed that he and Jessie would be spending that time together, and the fact that they are so obviously not doing that concerns me. I hope he hasn't fucked this up again. I'm not sure what more she can do to prove herself to him, but he is the most stubborn man I've ever met.

When Matt and Lisa are gone, I walk over to her, sitting on the bed in front of her. "Mikey and I can stay with Liam if you like," I offer.

"I know. But I want to stay too if that's okay?" she looks up at me, her eyes red from crying earlier. At least I hope it's from earlier.

"Of course you can. I just wondered if..." I shrug.

"What?" she blinks at me.

"Nothing, Angel," I say as I reach out and brush my fingertips over the cut on her cheek. "You look tired and it's been a long night. Why don't you climb in here with our boy and get some sleep?" I stand up and hold my hand out to her.

"You think it's okay for me to sleep in there with him? What if I hurt him?"

"Hurt him? You weigh like a third of what he does. And the bed is huge." I pull her up from the chair. "Besides, he will want you there when he wakes up." I lift the covers and indicate for her to get inside.

She nods and wipes a stray tear from her cheek and I think I'm going to strangle Shane when I get my hands on him, because she wasn't this upset ten minutes earlier. "My clothes are dirty," she says as she starts peeling off her jeans. I watch her slide them down her legs and have to remind my cock that this is not the time or the place.

"Here's a clean t-shirt, Red," Mikey says as he tosses one of his from the other side of the room.

"Thank you." She reaches out and catches it, placing it on the bed as she strips off the rest of her clothes. I have to avert my eyes from her incredible curves because my cock is already twitching. When she's ready, I lift the covers again, and she climbs into bed. She looks so vulnerable and fragile lying there in Mikey's t-shirt that dwarfs her frame, her eyes red and her cheek smeared with dried blood from the cut there. But I know she is neither of those things. She is a fucking warrior princess. Rightful head of the Bratva, and she would be a fucking good one too, but she walked away from it all to be a Ryan.

"Try to get some sleep, Angel. Mikey will stay here with you both."

"I'm just going to take a shower. But I'm right here if you need me, Red," he replies as he saunters to the bathroom.

"And what about you?" she asks as she stares up at me with those incredible blue eyes.

"I have some things I need to take care of. I'll be back later. Promise," I say before leaning down to give her a kiss. She wraps her arms around my neck as she kisses me back with so much need that I have to force myself not to climb on top of her and fuck her while my little brother lies two feet away in an opiate induced coma. I pull back from her with a groan. "Sleep. Now," I order and she gives me one of her incredible smiles before rolling onto her side and resting her hand lightly on Liam's.

After leaving the twins' bedroom, I go to find Shane. It's no surprise he's in his office, his head bent over his computer and a scowl on his face.

"Everything okay?" I ask when I step inside.

"Yeah," he snaps, not even bothering to look up at me.

"You sure?"

"Yeah."

"Really?" I say as I walk into the room and sit on the edge of his desk. "Cause it kind of seems like you're super pissed."

"I'm just busy. And tired." He looks up at me. "I've booked a plane to Chicago in the morning. I'm leaving first thing."

"Chicago? Why?" I frown at him.

"We just took out the head of the Bratva, Con. That will have consequences. I'll need to smooth a few things over, is all."

"You need me to come with you?"

"No," he shakes his head. "It's not that kind of business. It's our legitimate associations I'm worried about."

"Okay," I nod.

"Besides, I'll be gone for at least a week. I need you to take care of things here while I'm gone."

"A week? Fuck, Shane! Do you really need to be away that long?"

He glares at me. "You just took two months off chasing Jessie across the country, but I can't take a week to handle some business?" he snarls.

I hold my hands up in surrender. "I didn't mean it like that. We'll miss you, is all. But what the fuck has crawled up your ass?"

He turns away and puts his head in his hands, and I realize exactly what this is about.

"What happened between you two? I thought she'd be with you right now?"

"Yeah? Well, so did I."

"What? She turned you down? Jessie?"

He looks up at me. "Is that so hard to believe? That she is the one who is pushing me away and not the other way around."

"Yeah," I say with a frown. "Because that girl fucking adores you, Shane. So, what did you do?"

"Just forget it, Con. Jessie and I are done. We'll never be what you want us to be so, for the love of God, will you stop pushing me about it?" he snaps.

I resist the urge to ask him any more questions because it will only piss him off more. "You need me to do anything right now?" I ask instead.

"No. I've got a few phone calls to make, and them I'm going to pack and get some sleep. Tell Liam I'll call him tomorrow night some time. Okay?"

"Okay," I say with a sigh. I know he's not lying about having to smooth things over with some of our business associates, but I do wonder about whether he really has to leave so soon, or whether he is running away because he is terrified of confronting this thing between him and Jessie. But I wish the two of them would sort their drama out, because I fucking hate seeing him like this.

. . .

It's another three hours before I go back to Mikey and Liam's bedroom. I ended up staying in Shane's office and keeping him company before I helped him pack. I can't do anything about the situation between him and Jessie, but I can just be there for him. The way he always is for the rest of us.

The room is dark when I step inside and it takes a moment for my eyes to adjust. Jessie is still in bed with Liam, but Mikey is in there too, lying right behind her with his body pressed up against hers. Each of them with a hand on Liam. I have no idea what any of us would have done if we hadn't gotten Liam back safely, but especially Mikey. I swear either one of them would die without the other. I walk over to Mikey's bed and crawl beneath the covers, not even bothering to undress because I'm so damn tired. By the time the three of them wake up, Shane will be on a plane to Chicago and things are going to get real hectic around here, especially with Liam out of action too. So I guess I'd better sleep while I still can.

I close my eyes and can't help but smile as I listen to Liam's soft snoring. It reminds me of a time when he and Mikey were about fourteen and they had been grounded by Shane for smoking weed in the house. He has always been anti-drugs, which is kind of ironic given what we do. The twins snuck out of the house and went to a party. They stole two bottles of tequila from the bar that we owned back in Ireland, and drank almost an entire bottle each. Mikey managed to call me, although he could barely speak, and I went to pick them up. Mikey was drunk and could barely walk, but Liam had completely passed out and I had to carry him to the car and then into the house. I'd been so worried about him choking on his own vomit, that I'd kicked out the girl I had staying over and put him in my bed instead. And then I had to listen to him snore all night. Neither he or Mikey have ever touched tequila since. When Shane came home the following morning, the two of them looked so ill and sorry for themselves, that he couldn't even bring himself to punish them any further.

Mikey spent most of the day with his head in the toilet, while Liam had just lay on the sofa like a slug, puking into a bucket at half-hour intervals.

I chuckle to myself at the memory. We did have some good times when we were younger. Mostly when our father wasn't around. He'd been on one of his many trips to Spain that weekend. Even when our mom was alive, he'd disappeared there with one of his lady friends every couple of weeks. I think she looked forward to them, much like we all came to, because it offered some peace from him. If only he had fucked off to Spain permanently, all of our lives would have been a whole lot happier.

CHAPTER

TWELVE

JESSIE

It's the sensation of Liam's fingers twitching in my hand as I hold onto his gently that rouses me from my sleep.

"Jessie," he groans and I untangle myself from Mikey, who has an arm and a leg draped over me, and sit up.

"Hey, sunshine. How are you feeling?" I smile at him.

"Like I got run over by a fucking forty ton truck," he winces as he tries to sit up.

"Just lie still, and I'll get you something to drink." I glance at the clock and it's after 6am so he can have some more pain relief now. "I'll get your meds too."

He mumbles something unintelligible as I climb over Mikey so I can get out of bed, waking him too.

"This is really not appropriate while my brother is at death's door right next to us, Red," he says sleepily as he places his hands on my waist. I roll my eyes at him and try to climb off him, but he holds me in place.

"Hey!" Liam croaks from beside us. "Death sent me packing, didn't you hear?"

"Yeah, he couldn't handle you," Mikey chuckles as he sits up and lifts me off him and places me on the edge of the bed.

"He's awake," Conor says from the opposite side of the room and it's only then I notice that he has spent the night in here too.

"Yeah," Liam groans. "Fuck!" he shouts as he tries to sit up again.

"Will you stop trying to move?" I shout at him as I walk around to his side of the bed. "Dr. Lisa said complete bed rest."

"And I'll stay in bed, but I need to sit up," he moans.

"Fine! We'll help you, but just take it easy." I nod to Mikey and we take an arm each and carefully pull Liam into a sitting position while fixing his pillows. He winces in pain but he doesn't complain any further as we make him comfortable.

"You need to eat with these too. What can I get you?" I say as I shake two pills from the bottle, remembering what Lisa told me.

"I'm not hungry." He shakes his head.

"You have to eat something. Just a slice of toast?" I offer.

"No."

"Banana?"

"No," he pouts like a toddler.

"Well you don't get any meds then." I arch an eyebrow at him.

"I'm in pain!" he snaps.

"Do you want me to get Shane in here to force you to eat?" I challenge him.

At that, Liam looks around the room. "Where *is* Shane?" he frowns.

Conor clears his throat and we all look at him. "He's gone to Chicago," he says almost apologetically.

"Chicago?" Mikey says with a frown. "Why?"

"He needs to smooth some things over with a few of our business associates, given that we took out the head of the Bratva and all."

55

"But he just took off without telling any of us?" Mikey's frown turns to a scowl now as a knot of anxiety forms in the pit of my stomach. Did Shane leave because of me? I feel so guilty already for turning him away. He needed me and I wasn't there for him.

Conor glances at me and the look in his eyes tells me he knows. Did he and Shane talk about what happened last night? I drop my head so he doesn't see the tears in my eyes.

"I'm going to make you a piece of toast, Liam," I say without making eye contact with any of them, and then I walk out of the bedroom and make my way to the kitchen. I've only just left the room when I hear soft footsteps behind me, and I turn around to see Conor following me.

"You okay, Angel?" he asks as he catches up with me and slides an arm around my waist.

"Yeah," I say as I wipe the tears from my eyes.

"He just had something to take care of, that's all," he says softly, reading my mind the way that he can.

"I understand," I say with a nod. I don't want to talk about what happened between us last night. "But he didn't say goodbye to any of us."

Conor reaches into the pocket of his jeans and pulls out his cell phone, unlocking it with his fingerprint. "Here. Call him."

I shake my head. "He won't want to speak to me."

"You won't know that unless you call him," he checks his watch. "You'd better hurry though. His plane takes off in ten minutes."

I take the phone from Conor's hand. "Thank you."

"No problem. I'll go make a start on Liam's toast," he says with a wink, and I watch him walk down the hallway.

My fingers tremble as I dial Shane's number and wait for him to pick up.

"Hey, Con. What's up?" he says when he answers and he sounds so sad that my heart hurts.

"It's me," I say. "Conor gave me his phone to call you."

"Oh. What is it, Jessie?" he snaps, the coldness in his tone now.

"I just wanted to..." Damn! What do I want? To tell him that I'm sorry he thought he had to leave? That I'm sorry I didn't spend the night in his bed. But I'm not. That was the right thing for both of us, even if he doesn't see that.

"Wanted to what?" he asks, his voice softer now, but then I hear another voice in the background. A distinctive, female Irish voice. Damn Erin! Always waiting in the wings to pounce as soon as I step a foot out of line. Damn Shane too! Running to her just because I hurt his pride. Asshole!

"I didn't realize Erin was with you?" I say, willing him to tell me that I'm mistaken and that it's a stewardess who sounds exactly like her.

"There are some contracts I need her help with," he replies in that gravelly tone that usually makes my legs turn to jelly.

"Well, I hope the two of you have a pleasant trip. Looks like you'll get that itch scratched after all?" I snap.

"Bye, Jessie," he practically snarls the words.

I don't reply. I end the call and shake my head. I am a complete fool for feeling even an ounce of guilt for not being there when I thought he needed me. I take a deep breath and pull my shoulders back before I go to the kitchen and have to face Conor because I don't want him to see how much his asshole older brother has got to me. Shane Ryan can go to hell for all I care.

THIRTEEN

It's been two and a half days since we got Liam back home and two days since Shane left for his *business* trip with Erin. I have only spoken to him once and that was only to say hi and pass the phone to Liam. Even the few words we spoke were strained and uncomfortable. Conor keeps in regular contact with him. Not that I have seen much of Conor either. He and Mikey have been doing the work of four brothers with Shane gone and Liam out of action. At least Mikey sleeps in here with us, but Conor is like a ghost, drifting through the apartment to eat and sleep. I miss him. And Shane.

I look down at Liam's handsome face and smile as his eyelids flutter and he drifts off to sleep. He is my priority right now, and his recovery is more important than me missing his brothers' company. His injuries are healing well. Dr. Lisa says there will be no permanent scarring to his face, and only a little on his chest and back. Not that anything could make this man any less attractive to me. He is a beautiful soul. Inside and out.

"Is he asleep?" Mikey asks as he walks out of the bathroom with a towel wrapped around his waist and his skin glistening, still damp from his shower. He is the mirror image of his twin, but so very different in so many ways.

"Yes," I say as I brush Liam's hair from his face. It took me ages to wash all the blood from it, using just a bowl of water with shampoo and a washcloth, but now it is back to normal. Dark and thick. It's too long, and he needs a haircut because it keeps falling into his eyes. Although it does make him look downright adorable.

Mikey walks over to the bed and holds his hand out to me. "Let him sleep, Red."

I nod my agreement and push myself up, taking hold of Mikey's hand and allowing him to pull me up. Unexpectedly, he scoops me into his arms, making me giggle as he walks us to the other side of the room and places me down in the middle of his king-size bed.

I watch as he slides off his towel and dries his hair with it. When he's finished, his hair is sticking up all over the place and it makes me smile at him, and he gives me a goofy grin in return.

"You look after him so well, Red," he says as he smooths back his hair before lying on the bed beside me. "He's doing better than anyone thought he would. Even the doc said she is amazed at how well he's doing."

"Thank you. He deserves looking after," I say, thinking of all the trauma he has experienced in his life.

"He sure does," Mikey says as he brushes my hair back from my face. "And so do you."

"You guys always take care of me," I smile.

Mikey sucks the air in through his teeth. "Actually, I don't think you've been taken care of for a few days now." He arches one eyebrow at me.

"Oh," I whisper as the heat flushes between my thighs. "But, don't you have to go to work?"

"Yeah. But I have always have time for you. And I can be a little late," he grins. "I'm the boss."

"But Liam is sleeping," I remind him.

"Well, you had better be quiet then, Red," he winks at me before rolling on top of me. "Besides, those meds he's on knock him out for hours."

"You're a bad man, Mikey Ryan."

"Well, you're a fucking hot woman, Jessie Ryan, and I really need to fuck you. Like now," he growls as he holds himself up on one powerful forearm while his free hand snakes down my body and slips into my panties.

"Mikey," I groan softly as his hand travels lower until he brushes the pad of two fingers over my clit.

"Jessie," he chuckles, teasing me as he moves his head lower, sucking on my hard nipple through the fabric of my top as he toys with my clit before he nudges my thighs apart with his knee. His fingers travel further south until his entire hand is fisting in my panties and I groan loudly when he pushes a finger inside me. "Oh, you're so fucking wet already, Red," he groans as he pulls his hand free and begins to tug my panties roughly down my legs. "Let's get these off you so I can make you come nice and hard," he growls before tossing them onto the floor. Then he moves further down the bed, bending his head low and licking the length of my pussy. "Fuck! You are so fucking sweet. I love eating you out."

I run my fingers through his hair as the familiar waves of pleasure start building in my stomach and thighs. It has been too long since I have felt him there. He licks and sucks me as pushes a second finger inside my pussy and I raise my hips up to meet him, desperate for the orgasm that he is about to deliver.

"You're so easy," he chuckles softly, the sound vibrating through me and adding to my pleasure.

"Mikey?" I plead.

"You want to come, Red?"

"Yes," I moan loudly, no longer concerned about Liam across the room. It's not like he hasn't seen this plenty of times before anyway.

Mikey curls the tips of his fingers inside me, pressing against that sweet spot as he grazes my clit with his teeth, and I come quickly and loudly. When he pulls his fingers out of me, a rush of my cum follows, making my face flush with heat.

"You are a bad girl, Red," he grins at me and I stare up at him, chewing on my lip as the last of my climax ebbs away. He leans down, pressing his lips over mine and kissing me fiercely, and I taste myself on him. I groan into his mouth as he pulls up my tank top up, breaking our kiss to work it off over my head.

"I am so desperate to fuck you," he groans before pushing himself up on his knees and flipping me over and pulling me up until I'm on all fours. He slaps my ass and I squeal. "You want this?" he growls as he pushes the tip of his cock inside me.

"Yes," I pant as I push back against him, but he edges back too, teasing me. "Please, Mikey?" I gasp.

"I love to hear you beg," he chuckles as he grabs me by the hips and then drives his cock deep inside me. I throw my head back as the euphoria courses through me at the sensation of him filling me, and the rush of wet heat between my thighs makes my legs tremble.

"You're so fucking tight, Red. I love pounding my cock into your pussy," he hisses as he rails into me. I lean forward, pressing my face into the pillow to muffle my groans as he reaches around to my clit and begins to rub, bringing me to the edge again.

He leans forward, wrapping my hair around his free hand and pulling me back against him, until my back is flush with his chest. This is one of his favorite positions, and mine. It allows him to suck on my neck and also gives him easier access to the rest of my body. "Don't hide that beautiful mouth. I want to hear every single fucking sound you make when you come for me," he growls.

"Oh God, Mikey," I hiss as he drives into me over and over again. Peppering kisses on my throat as he holds my head back by my hair and rubs delicious circles over my clit with his free hand. A few seconds later, I cry out as my climax crashes over me. He growls something unintelligible in my ear as he grinds out his own and fills me with his cum.

After we have caught our breath, he pulls out of me and I fall forward onto the bed, gasping for breath. Mikey lies down on top of me, supporting his weight on his forearms as he presses a soft kiss between my shoulder blades. "I wish I could stay here with you all night, Red. But I really got to get to work."

"I know," I sigh contentedly.

"Take care of my baby brother for me," he says before he pushes himself up and climbs off the bed and I shiver at the loss of his warmth.

Pulling the covers over myself, I turn on my side and watch him dress. He has an incredible body, and he fills his tailored suit like he was born to wear it. My stomach flutters at the sight of him as he fixes his cufflinks and straightens his shirt. He turns to grab his jacket and catches me staring at him.

"You enjoying the show?" he asks with a grin as he walks back toward the bed.

I roll onto my back and smile up at him. "I sure am," I say with a sigh as I lick my lips. "It is quite the show after all. You almost look better in that suit than you do out of it."

"Don't, Jessie," he says with a growl and a shake of his head as he reaches me.

"Don't what?" I flutter my eyelashes at him.

"Don't make me later for work than I already am," he narrows his eyes at me.

"I'm not sure what you mean. I'm just lying here watching you dress." I give him my sweetest smile and he sits on the bed beside me, running his hand over the covers, up the outside of my thigh and over my hip before settling on my stomach. He splays his huge hand over my abdomen, and I glance down at it and think about the wonderful things he can do with those fingers.

"I know what you're thinking, Red, and it's not happening," he chuckles before he leans down and gives me a soft kiss on the lips.

"I was thinking that I should take a shower and get some sleep." I arch an eyebrow at him.

"Sure you were. Just like I was thinking I should really get to work and stop touching you," he winks at me. "But you should get some sleep."

"And you should get to work. Conor will be wondering where you are."

He nods and brushes the back of his knuckles across my cheek. "I'll see you in the morning."

"See you then," I reach out and take his hand, wanting to prolong this moment with him. He stares down at me as though he's trying to read my mind. "I love you," I whisper.

"Love you too, Jessie," he gives me a final kiss on the cheek before standing up and walking out of the room.

FOURTEEN

I took a long, hot shower and climbed into bed with Liam after Mikey left, and it didn't take me long to fall asleep. The warmth of a rough hand rubbing over the skin on my hip rouses me as I lie curled up next to Liam.

"I've missed you so much," Conor groans against my ear as he presses his body against mine.

"I've missed you too, bro," Liam pipes up beside us, making me giggle and Conor laugh.

"How you doing, kid?" Conor asks him as he lifts his head from my neck.

"Feel like I've been run over by a freight train, but other than that, all good," he groans as he shifts his position slightly. "And I got the hottest nurse in the world looking after me, so you know. Silver linings and all."

Conor is pressing a soft kiss against my shoulder blade. "Hmm," he murmurs against my skin. "Some of us are busting our asses while you're laying in bed all day getting sponge baths from Jessie," he teases.

"Yeah, I'm living the dream," Liam chuckles, but the effort makes him wince in pain, and he holds onto his ribs.

"Are you okay?" I ask him as Conor continues distracting me by peppering my shoulders and neck with kisses.

"Yeah," he says as he reaches for my hand and curls his fingers gingerly around my own.

"Good," I kiss his bicep softly as I press my hips back against Conor and realize he's naked when his cock presses against the seam of my ass through my panties.

"Fuck, you feel so good, Angel," Conor growls as his hand slides beneath my tank and onto my stomach, causing the wet heat to surge between my thighs.

"Con," Liam groans. "Could you please not fuck Jessie right now?"

I bite my lip and Conor tenses behind me, his hand splayed across my abdomen as he pulls me closer to him. Liam has never objected to us fooling around or fucking in front of him before. "I'm going to get a raging, painful boner listening to her moaning in my ear while you make her come, and there is fuck all I can do about it right now."

I bite down on my lip to stifle a giggle while Conor sighs dramatically. "Fine," he growls. "But you owe me big time. I got a raging boner here of my own right now."

"Well, I'm not averse to Jessie giving you a hand job. Your groans I can handle, just not hers," he says as he brushes the pad of his thumb over my fingertips.

"Do I get any say in this at all?" I ask as I snuggle between the two of them. "I'm kinda tired too, you know?"

"Then stop wiggling that fine ass against me, and go back to sleep, Angel," Conor whispers in my ear as he wraps his arms around me. "I'm beat, anyway."

"Then you should get some sleep too," I breathe as I close my eyes and squeeze my thighs together to try and stop the throbbing in my pussy.

Five minutes later, I'm listening to the sound of Liam's soft snores and Conor's steady breathing behind me. Damn! I'm wide awake now, and sandwiched between two sleeping giants and there is not a thing I can do about the growing need that starts burning through my body. It has been days since Conor and I have been intimate, but it seems like it's been an eternity.

I bite down on my lip and close my eyes. Just go to sleep, Jessie!

It's then that Conor moves his hand and his fingertips twitch on my stomach before he slowly slides his hand lower until they slip beneath the waistband of my panties.

I suck in a breath, and he presses his lips against my ear. "Shh!" he warns softly.

I nod my understanding and clamp my lips together as his fingers slip between my thighs and he begins to toy with my clit. His movements are slow in order to not disturb Liam, but they are precise, and it's not long before my thighs are trembling with my impending release. This man is a magician with his hands and he has me on the edge of oblivion despite him hardly even moving. I try to rock my hips up into his hand, but he holds me firmly in place with my ass pressed against his rock hard cock.

I can barely stand his maddening torment any longer when he increases the pressure and pace at the same time and I have to turn my head and bite down on the pillow as my orgasm rolls over me in wave after delicious wave while Conor continues working me with his expert fingers.

As the last of it subsides, I finally lift my face from the pillow and take in a deep breath just as Conor pulls my panties down over my ass until they're resting at the top of my thighs. I close my eyes as his cock nudges against me, because I'm pretty sure there's no way I'm going to be able to stay quiet if he fucks me. He obviously knows that too because the next thing I feel is his huge hand clamped firmly over my mouth as he begins to suck on the tender spot on my neck that he knows drives me crazy. His fingers are damp with my release and I smell myself on them, which makes this even hotter. He edges closer, pressing the tip of his cock against my opening and making me groan against his palm as my whole body trembles in anticipation.

He presses his lips against my ear. "Shh," he soothes as he pushes all the way inside me and the soft moan, a mixture of relief and pleasure, vibrates through my whole body as he holds me in place. He moves slowly, gently thrusting in and out of me and causing the pleasure to course through my veins.

"Can you be quiet if I move my hand?" he whispers.

I shake my head. There is no way that's going to happen. His hand is the only thing preventing me from shouting his name down Liam's ear.

He chuckles softly. "I've missed this hot pussy, Angel. I wish I could spread you wide open and taste you. I want to fuck you real hard because it's been a fucking lifetime since I've been inside you. I want to fuck you like you deserve, but this will have to do for now," he growls quietly, and my insides turn to molten lava. I have missed him too. I can hardly believe that it was less than a week ago that we got back from our road trip from Arizona. Five days and four nights together and it was heaven. We got so close, but since we got back, we've had no time alone together. And Liam has to be my priority right now, and I know that Conor understands that too, but it still doesn't stop us from missing this closeness. I need him, and his brothers, like I need air.

As Conor rocks his hips, fucking me with only the slightest of movements, he hits that sweet spot deep inside me that makes my eyelids flutter and my insides contract. My walls squeeze around him as I fall over the edge again and the sound of his soft groan against my neck tells me he has fallen straight over with me.

When my breathing starts to return to normal and my climax has ebbed away, Conor pulls his hand from my mouth, turning my head as he does, he presses a soft kiss on my lips as he pulls my panties back up, patting my ass when he's done before pressing his body back up against me. He wraps his huge arm around me again and nuzzles my neck and I smile in contentment.

CHAPTER

FIFTEEN

JESSIE

When I wake up a few hours later, Conor is no longer in bed with me, and I can't help but feel a little sad. It was nice falling asleep with his arms wrapped around me. I miss spending time with him. I don't have time to dwell on why he left, because Liam shifts beside me and groans loudly.

"Morning, handsome," I say, stretching and rolling out of bed. "How are you feeling?"

"Like a truck rolled over me in the night," he winces as he rolls his shoulders and stretches before hoisting himself into a sitting position.

"I'll grab you something to eat, and then you can have some of your pain meds."

"Thanks, baby," he says with a grimace as I walk around to his side of the bed and start clearing his nightstand.

"Conor fucked you, didn't he?" he arches an eyebrow at me.

I bite on my lip. "Yes," I whisper. "Sorry."

He chuckles softly. "No need to be sorry, baby. I just didn't want to hear you coming down my ear, is all. I mean, usually it's pretty fucking hot, but not while I'm out of commission."

69

I sit on the bed beside him. "How did you know?" I frown at him.

He places his hand on my inner thigh, and stretches out his index finger. "Your panties are wet," he says with a devilish grin as he runs the tip over the fabric at the apex of my thighs and the blush creeps over my cheeks. "I mean, you're pretty much always wet, baby, but they are soaked."

"Oh," I breathe.

"I can't wait to be the one to soak them with you again," he winks at me and I laugh.

"I'll just clean up and then I'll go make you some breakfast," I say as I climb off the bed and walk to the bathroom.

"No rush. I'm not that hungry," he yawns.

LIAM HAS FALLEN BACK ASLEEP by the time I've taken a quick shower. He looks so peaceful and pain free when he's sleeping, but I will have to make him some breakfast and wake him soon so he can take his pain meds. I grab my cell phone and walk out of his bedroom, taking a quick detour to my own.

I sit on my bed, and my stomach is in knots as I dial the number. I'm not even sure if he will have kept the same number, especially now that he's had a significant promotion. The phone rings out and I swallow hard as I wait for it to be answered. I am about to hang up when I hear his distinctive Russian voice.

"Jessica?"

"Jessie," I remind him.

"Of course," he clears his throat. "What can I do for you?"

"I..." I take a deep breath. "I still have so many questions, Vlad. About my parents. About Alexei. About the Wolf. I've tried to move on from my past, but I can't let it go."

"I understand that," he replies softly.

"Do you have any of the answers I need?"

There is a few seconds' silence before he replies. "About your family? Perhaps. About the Wolf? No."

I suck in another deep breath. "Do you think we could meet?"

"Are you sure that is wise? I'm not sure your new family would be too happy about that," he warns, and I know that's true. But he is my only link to my past, and I have to understand who I really am and where I came from.

"You're right. But they'll understand. Please, Vlad? I'm just asking for one hour of your time."

He sighs deeply. "I will be in New York later today. Perhaps we could meet then?"

"Yes," I reply almost before he has finished speaking. "Where?"

"Somewhere out in the open," he says.

"Of course," I agree. He is the head of the Bratva now, and for all he truly knows, this could be a trap. "Central Park. Near the zoo?"

"Yes. Just you?"

"Yes," I reply. "I'll come alone."

"Lád-na. I will be there at noon."

"Lád-na." *Deal.* I smile. "And thank you, Vlad."

"Pozhaluysta." *You're welcome.*

CHAPTER
SIXTEEN

JESSIE

After hanging up the call to Vlad, I tuck my cell into my jeans and walk to the kitchen to find Mikey and Conor sitting at the breakfast bar eating cereal, and I wander over to them. I reach Conor first and he pulls me between his powerful thighs, brushing my hair back from my face and holding me in place as he bends his head to kiss me. Wrapping my arms around his waist, I melt into his kiss and moan softly as the warmth floods my core, making Mikey chuckle. I swear these men turn me into a sex addict.

"You left without waking me this morning?" I breathe when he lets me up for air.

With a lick of his lips, he grins at me and drops one hand to my ass, squeezing hard. "I couldn't lie there any longer with this juicy ass pressed up against me and not fuck you, Angel. And Liam needs his rest."

I look up into his eyes, noticing how red they are. "So do you," I remind him. "You're working too hard."

"No such thing," he winks at me. "Anyway, I just came in here to catch up with Mikey and then I'm off to bed. Maybe you can join me later?"

"I would love to," I purr as I run my hands down his hard chest and then I turn to Mikey. "Are you going to be around all day today?"

"Sure am, Red," he says as he shovels in another spoonful of Lucky Charms. "You got something planned?"

"Yes, actually. I need to go out for a few hours. I can take one of the cars, right?"

Conor tightens his grip on me. "Of course you can take a car, Angel. You don't have to ask. But where are you going?"

I bite my lip. They aren't going to like this, but it's something I need to do. "I'm going to see Vlad."

I barely get the last word out of my mouth when Conor is interrupting me. "The fuck you are. Not a chance, Jessie," he snarls with a shake of his head.

"I agree, Red. No way you're going there," Mikey chimes in unhelpfully.

I swallow the frustration and resist the urge to remind them that I'm a grown woman who looked after herself for ten long years before they came into my life, because we have been through so much these past few months, and I understand their concern. So, instead I take a deep breath. "I knew you'd both think it was a bad idea, but don't you see that I have to do this? Vlad might have some answers for me, about my parents, about Alexei. Maybe even about the Wolf. I need to find out what he knows."

"No!" Conor snaps.

"He might not even want to talk to you," Mikey adds.

"He will. I spoke to him just now," I reply.

"What the fuck?" Conor shouts, releasing me from his grip and standing up so he is towering over me. "You've been talking to Vlad?"

"Yes. I called him. I understand what Alexei did, and I get that you don't trust the Russians, but I believe that Vlad is a man of his word. We're meeting in Central Park, for Christ's sake. We're just going to talk. I swear."

"No fucking way, Jessie," Conor growls as he runs a hand through his hair. "I'm not discussing this any further."

"Conor!" I shout, glaring at him. "How can you deny me learning the truth about my family? Please try and see this from my point of view?"

He moves so fast that I gasp in surprise. He wraps one of his large hands around my throat, pushing me against the counter, the weight of his body holding me in place as he leans his face close to mine. "Why don't you see it from mine?" he hisses. "I will not fucking lose you again."

I swallow, and he loosens his grip slightly. "You won't. I promise," I whisper.

"How about I go with her?" Mikey offers.

"And have to worry about the two of you all day? No!" he shakes his head.

"Conor! Please?" I beg. I had planned on going alone, and I told Vlad that I would, but it seems there is no way Conor will let me and maybe having Mikey as a chaperone might persuade him, because I wouldn't put it past him to lock me in my room. I had known they wouldn't be pleased with my decision, but I hadn't expected this level of anger from him. "I trust Vlad. We're meeting in a public place and if you insist I have a body-guard, then Mikey will come with me. I need to know about my past. Everything I believed about my parents was a lie. Don't you think I deserve the truth?"

Conor's eyes momentarily flick to his brother before he releases my throat from his grip and slides his hand to the back of my neck instead. "I don't trust him," he says as he presses his forehead against mine. "Why do you have to do this right now?"

"Because I have been searching for answers for ten years, and I'm done waiting," I breathe.

The sigh comes from deep inside his chest, and I shiver as his breath skitters over my cheek. "I want you both back here within two hours. You understand me?"

I glance sideways at Mikey, who winks at me and I smile. "Yes, of course. Thank you."

TWO HOURS LATER, Mikey and I make our way through Central Park to the place I've agreed to meet Vlad. I see his distinctive figure ahead and scan the crowd for signs of his bodyguards. Mikey spots him too and does the same.

"You recognize any of his goons, Red?" he asks as he looks around.

"Not really. But there's a guy leaning against that tree and another one near the hotdog stand that scream Bratva to me. What do you think?"

Mikey narrows his eyes as he checks out the two men I just mentioned, and then he nods. "I agree, Red. Let's hope they're only here to keep an eye on their boss and not to start any trouble, because Conor will have my ass if anything goes down here this afternoon."

I take hold of his hand, entwining my fingers through his. "Relax. The head of the Bratva doesn't go anywhere without bodyguards. You know that."

He lifts my hand to his lips and kisses my knuckles. "Let's do this then, Red," he says with a grin as we make our way over to Vlad.

Vlad smiles at me as I approach him before giving Mikey a once over. Mikey releases my hand. "I'll give you some space, Red. But I'll be two steps behind you."

"Thank you," I whisper before turning and making my way over to Vlad.

"Good afternoon, Jessie," he says in his thick Russian accent.

"Afternoon, Vlad. I had to bring Mikey with me, but he's good. Thank you for agreeing to meet with me."

He nods and draws in a deep breath. "Of course. Shall we walk?" he holds out his arm and I take it by the elbow. Although he towers over me and is almost twice my size, there is something about him that makes me feel at ease and I imagine he is a much easier man to work for than my father ever was. We start to walk and Mikey falls into step a few yards behind us. Vlad puts his free hand over mine and I notice his wedding ring for the first time. I'm sure he never wore it when I was at Alexei's house.

"You're married, Vlad?"

He pats my hand gently and smiles. "Yes. Twenty-seven years."

Something about that endears him to me even more.

"Children?" I press.

"Two sons," he says with a nod toward the hot dog stand as we pass. "Grown men. They accompany me everywhere now."

"And your wife?"

"Well, she doesn't handle a Beretta in quite the same way," he laughs softly.

"I meant what does she do?" I laugh too.

"Time is precious, Jessie. I suspect you didn't persuade me to meet you here in New York to discuss my family. So, tell me what it is you want to know?"

I nod my head. He's right. This isn't a catch up with an old friend. This is an information gathering exercise, and I need to get this done because Conor will lose his shit if Mikey and I aren't back by the time we promised. "I want to learn about my parents, Vlad. My real parents. What the hell happened to make them change their names and flee to the States?"

He clears his throat before he speaks. "You know, I knew your father when he was just a boy. Him and Alexei. His name was Boris then, and not Peter, of course, but my father worked for theirs and we grew up like cousins."

"So, you knew him well?" My heart lurches in my chest that I might finally get some answers.

"Hmm. A very long time ago. And your mother too."

"Tell me what happened? Please?"

"I can tell you all I know, but to tell you about your parents, I must also tell you about Alexei. Their story is his too."

I nod and close my eyes. "I want to know everything."

"Your father was always the smart one while Alexei was much more outgoing and confident — arrogant some would say. Boris was your grandmother's favorite, and she protected him from the darker side of living with the Bratva, but Alexei thrived at his father's side, and all of the darker personality traits that he possessed were encouraged and nurtured by the life he was forced to live. He was the perfect choice to take over when your grandfather died."

"So, he and my father didn't get along as children then?"

Vlad shakes his head and sucks in the air through his teeth. "On the contrary, Jessie, despite their differences, they were as close as two brothers have ever been. By the time Alexei was a man, he was uncontrollable, but your father was always the one man who could reach him. He was the only man who could keep Alexei in line, and the only person whose counsel he would heed. They shared an unbreakable bond. At least it appeared that way, until Alexei met your mother."

My mom! A wave of sadness and nostalgia washes over me. I miss her so much. "So Alexei met her first?"

Vlad nods as we continue walking through the park.

"How did they meet?"

He smiles and the corners of his eyes crinkle softly. "At the opera."

"The opera?"

"Yes. Your father was supposed to go with your grand-mother, but he was ill with the flu, so Alexei accompanied her instead. Your mother was there with her father." He turns to me at this point and studies my face. "She was a true beauty," he says, reaching out and brushing his fingertips over my cheek. "As soon as Alexei saw her, he decided he wanted her, and that was that. The fact that she was the daughter of one of the wealthiest and most influential men in Russia meant nothing once the head of the Ivanov empire set his sights on her."

"So, what happened?"

Vlad sucks in a long breath and glances behind us. Mikey still follows closely behind, as well as his sons who keep a more discreet distance than my own bodyguard. "It is a very long story for some other time, but Alexei wanted her to be his wife, so she became his wife. She had no family other than her father, and he died a few months after their union. Alexei was always a cruel man, and I don't expect that he was able to hide his true nature from her."

I blink back the tears as I think about my mother being ripped from her life and forced to marry the head of the Bratva. How terrified and alone she must have felt with no family around her. "But her and my father?"

Vlad nods solemnly. "I don't know when that started, but your mother and father must have fallen in love. I didn't often see them spend any time in each other's company, but I recall one dinner when I caught the two of them sharing a look that made the hairs on the back of my neck stand on end." He shud-ders slightly at the memory.

"Why?"

"It was the look of two people so deeply in love that they would risk everything to be together, Jessie. I knew that it would bring trouble, and it did. But at the time, I tried to pretend it was all in my imagination. I convinced myself that Boris would never do that to his brother. Then she fell pregnant and Alexei was the happiest I've ever seen him. He threw a massive ball in Nataliya's honor. He commissioned portraits of him and his pregnant wife. He boasted to everyone he met that he was about to become a father. But a few weeks later, your mother and Boris disappeared."

I swallow. "How did Alexei react?"

"As you'd expect," he shrugs. "Like a crazed madman would. He tortured anyone with any allegiance, be it perceived or genuine, to your parents. He tore the country apart trying to find them. He searched for sixteen years before he found you all."

"And then he had the Wolf slaughter his own brother and his family?" I snap as the bile burns the back of my throat.

"Any flicker of humanity that Alexei held in his heart was snuffed out by the betrayal of the people he loved most in the world."

"You think it was their fault he was such a monster?" I challenge him.

He shrugs. "No judgment. I am simply stating the truth, Jessie."

He picks up his pace slightly and squeezes my arm tighter, and I sense the tension in Mikey, even though he's a few yards behind me.

"I don't have much more time. We must walk and talk faster," he adds with a reassuring smile.

"Sure," I nod. "Did Alexei ever meet the Wolf?"

"No," Vlad shakes his head. "Nobody has ever seen the Wolf and lived. Nobody except you, Jessie."

"So, he was supposed to deliver me to Alexei?"

"Yes, and when he didn't, Alexei almost lost his mind. All of those years searching for you, only to have you stolen from him by the very man he paid to bring you back."

"So, he searched for the Wolf too?"

"Vigorously." Vlad nods. "But there was never a trace of either of you. I tried to persuade Alexei that you were both dead. There seemed to be no other plausible explanation. But, well, now I realize that the Wolf is as good as the myths surrounding him suggest."

"You think he's still alive?" I ask.

"Yes," Vlad states and my heart sinks through my chest. I believe he is too, but hearing someone like Vlad say that too is like confirmation that I'm not crazy.

"I do too," I say quietly.

Vlad places his hand over mine and squeezes tightly. "I must go now."

"One more question?" I ask.

"Of course," he nods.

"Why didn't Alexei have me killed too? Why was he so sure I was his daughter if my parents were having an affair?"

"Oh, you were his daughter." Vlad narrows his eyes at me.

"But how could he know that? Even a DNA test couldn't determine the truth if he and my father were identical twins."

"True. But you were conceived while Boris was in prison."

"My dad? In prison? For what?"

Vlad shakes his head. "Some charge relating to espionage that nobody ever quite got to the bottom of. At the time, Alexei made noises about how unjust it was and how nobody put an Ivanov behind bars. He made everyone believe that it was he who got your father out. But, now I think that it was he who put your father in prison."

"He could do that?"

80

Vlad laughs softly. "In Russia, the head of the Bratva can do as he pleases."

"How did he get out then?"

"I believe Alexei did get him out. He loved your father very much. He was not the same man when Boris wasn't around. I suspect he believed that once your mother was pregnant with his child, that would put an end to any feelings between his wife and his brother."

"But it obviously didn't. And my father always treated me the same as my younger brothers. I had no inkling at all that I wasn't his biological child," I say as another rush of emotion almost floors me and I wipe a stray tear from my cheek.

"I appreciate that Alexei did terrible things, and hurt you badly, Jessie. But understand that in his own way, he loved you above all others."

I stare at him, searching his face. I am convinced that my instincts are right and I can trust this man. "Is that why you helped him take me from the Ryan brothers?"

His eyes narrow and darken. "Yes," he says solemnly. "I thought it was for the best. I didn't realize he was going to drug you."

"Why did he?"

"He was terrified that you would discover he wasn't the father you knew. He wanted you to discover his side of the story, I suppose, and he needed time to make you dependent on him. To force you to need him. For him, need equaled love."

"So, how did he find me?"

"This is more than one question, Jessie," he says as he checks his watch.

"Last one. Promise."

He stops in his tracks and turns to me, brushing a strand of hair from my face. "You are so very like her," he whispers. "In so many ways."

I smile at him, although I'm not sure if he means that as a compliment, but I will take it as one anyway, because my mom was the most amazing woman I ever knew.

"One of Dmitry's men, Viktor, recognized your mother in you. I was contacted by a nurse at the hospital, who told me that he was desperate to speak to Alexei because he'd found his daughter. I visited him there, and he told me what happened at that bar before I ended his suffering. It didn't take long to figure out who you were with. Future tip, Jessie. If you're trying to lie low, don't run around with the Irish Mafia." He cocks an eyebrow at me.

"Well, I kinda think that ship has sailed, don't you?"

He laughs softly. "You take good care of yourself, Jessie Ryan."

"I will. Thank you, Vlad."

He lifts my hand to his lips and kisses it softly before placing his free hand over his heart. "It has been my pleasure."

Before I can reply, his two sons are by his side talking to him in Russian. Vlad releases my hand and the three of them slip into the crowd as Mikey steps up beside me.

"You okay, Red?" he asks as he slides an arm around my waist.

I turn to him and smile. "Yes." I lean against his shoulder as we start to head back through the park. "I think I got most of the answers I needed. Thank you for coming with me, Mikey," I say, relieved now that he offered to be my chaperone, because I feel so emotional and vulnerable that it is comforting to have his huge arm wrapped around me.

"Any time, Red," he replies before planting a kiss on the top of my head.

"I love you," I breathe. "You know that?"

"Yeah," he says with a shrug, making me laugh.

"Did you hear any of that?"

"Most of it."

"It's so much to take in."

"I bet it is, Red. You want to go somewhere? Just the two of us?" he asks as he squeezes me tighter.

"I would love to. But Liam needs his lunch and his meds. Conor will probably be pacing the hallway, and even if he's not, you're well aware he won't sleep until we're back. Even if we call him and tell him we're okay."

"Okay," he says with an overly dramatic sigh, and I laugh again.

"How about we do something later? Just me and you?"

"Hmm," he says as he chews on his lip as if deep in thought. "How about strip poker?"

"Is your mind always in the gutter, Mikey Ryan?"

"Pretty much, Red," he laughs.

"Good. That's exactly where I like it," I laugh too.

"So, we're on for strip poker then?" he turns to me and smiles widely.

"Yes," I nod.

"Nice," he nods too before leaning down to give me a soft kiss on the lips. Mikey is my happy place. He has a unique ability to lighten any mood and uses humor to diffuse almost every situation, even when it's completely inappropriate. But that's one of the things I love about him. I know that beneath it all, he has a heart as big as anyone I've ever known. And as we walk toward the car, he leans down and whispers softly, "I love you too, Red."

CHAPTER
SEVENTEEN

CONOR

I'm half asleep when I feel the covers lifting slightly and the bed dipping beside me. I am fucking exhausted, but I'm conscious Liam might need something so my body won't let me fall into a deep sleep. And I've been worrying about Jessie and Mikey and won't be okay until they are back here where they belong. I trust Jessie's judgment, but I will never trust the Bratva. Not ever.

Her warm hand skims my lower abdomen and I smile because they are back — and safe.

"Hey, Angel."

"Hey you," she replies as she snuggles against me and I lift my arm so I can wrap it around her and she nestles into the crook of my shoulder. "I'm sorry I woke you but I've missed you these past few days."

"You didn't wake me. I was waiting for you to come home." I yawn. "And I've missed you too. Did everything go okay?"

"Yes. But I'll tell you about it later. Go back to sleep."

"Hmm." I pull her closer to me and she drapes her thigh over my legs. "You sure you don't want anything else from me?" I ask, even though I'm not sure where I'll find the energy from, but I will find some for her if that's what she needs.

"No," she breathes against my skin. "I just want to lie here with you. Is that okay?"

"Yes." I kiss the top of her head. "Sounds perfect. But if you could get naked, that would be even better."

"Behave yourself and go to sleep," she says, but I feel her smile against my chest.

"Yes, ma'am," I mumble. I close my eyes and she strokes the back of my neck with her index finger and I smile too because she knows my body as well as I know hers. I'm fast asleep a few seconds later.

JESSIE IS GONE by the time I wake up. Glancing at the clock, I see I've been asleep for five hours, so no doubt she will have needed to tend to Liam during that time. I roll out of bed and make my way to the kitchen, where I find her and Mikey making sandwiches.

She smiles when I walk into the room. "You want something to eat?" she asks.

I resist the temptation to tell her than I'd like to eat her. "Yes, please," I say instead as I sit at the island and watch them work. "What are we having?"

"Chicken, bacon and avocado," she replies.

"How many do you want, bro?" Mikey asks.

"As many as there are available. I'm starving," I reply as my stomach growls in agreement. Jessie brings a plate over to me with one sandwich and I look at it and frown. "Just to get you started," she laughs. "Did you have a good sleep?"

"Yep," I say as I stretch my arms and roll my neck. "Would have been better if I'd woken up with you still wrapped around me like a blanket though," I say quietly and she blushes.

"Sorry. But I had to give Liam his meds and some food. He needs to eat little and often with them," she whispers.

I reach out and pull her around the island until she's standing between my thighs. "I know, Angel. Liam needs to be your focus right now. But that doesn't mean I don't miss waking up next to you."

"I miss waking up next to you too," she breathes.

"As soon as I get a night off from the club, I am taking you to bed and locking the door behind us." I wink at her and she blushes again, but I imagine for an altogether different reason.

"Sounds good to me."

"Here you go, Red," Mikey walks over to us and hands her a tray.

"I have to take Liam his dinner," she says with a sweet smile.

"I'll catch you later, Angel," I say before I wrap my arms around her. I press my lips against hers and coax them open so I can push my tongue inside. She tastes so sweet. Of strawberries and Gatorade. Pressing her face closer to mine, I deepen our kiss until she is moaning into my mouth and my cock stiffens. I am desperate to fuck her properly. This morning wasn't enough, and it has already been too long since I've been inside her, but she needs to take care of Liam and I need to speak to Mikey.

As soon as Jessie has walked out of the kitchen, Mikey sits on the stool opposite me.

"So, how did it go?" I ask before taking a bite out of my sandwich.

"As well as can be expected, I think. Vlad had his two sons with him, but there was nothing untoward going on as far as I could tell. He gave her some of the answers she was looking for, and I think she thinks it was worthwhile. So, I suppose it was a success?"

"Good. He told her about her parents then?"

"Yep. Her father's real name was Boris. He fell in love with her mother, even though she was married to Alexei..."

"Oh? So they had an affair?" I had assumed that Alexei was the one who betrayed them and not the other way around.

"Well, yeah. But it kind of seemed like Jessie's mom didn't have much choice in marrying Alexei, if you know what I mean?"

"Hmm," I mumble with a mouthful of food.

"It was strange hearing about Alexei and Boris, though." Mikey shakes his head.

"Why?"

"Well, with them being twins? I assumed they must have always been rivals or had a difficult relationship, but according to Vlad, they were real close. Until Jessie's mom anyway."

"Why is that strange?" I frown at him.

"Well, it's not. It was just weird thinking about me and Liam, you know? There would never be anything he could ever do that would make me turn on him like that. And Vlad said that Alexei loved Jessie's mom too, but he still had her and Boris slaughtered?" he shakes his head again.

"Well, Alexei and you are very different people, Mikey," I remind him.

"I guess so," he says, but he seems distracted.

"What is it?"

"I was just thinking, is all," he replies with a shrug.

"Thinking what?"

"What if Jessie chose one of us? Like decided she fell in love with one of us more than the others? What would we do?"

I blink at him because that thought has never crossed my

mind, but it is a terrifying one. "I don't have a clue, bro," I answer honestly. "You think she would?"

He stares at me for a few seconds as though he's deep in thought. "Nah," he eventually says with a grin. "She can't get enough of us Ryans, can she?"

"Well, let's hope it stays that way." I force a smile because now he's got me thinking the same thing.

"You sure you can manage without me tonight, bro?" Mikey asks as he slips off his stool and goes back to the counter to make more sandwiches.

"Yeah. You deserve a night off."

"So do you." He turns and frowns at me. "Let the manager and the bouncers handle things tonight. Play strip poker with me and Jessie?"

"Strip poker?" I laugh.

"Yep." He grins and flashes his eyebrows. "Winner gets to choose their reward."

"As fun as that sounds, we have too much going on right now. I can't afford to take my eye off the ball, Mikey."

He shakes his head and sighs before turning his back on me again.

"I'll take some time off as soon as Shane is home and things calm down a little."

"Things are never calm around here, Con," he says, and I know he's right. But I can't slack off right now when Shane asked me to keep everything running smoothly. As much as I truly would prefer to spend my evening with a naked Jessie.

CHAPTER
EIGHTEEN
JESSIE

T step out of the elevator and make my way through the basement to the club. It's not open yet, but Conor is down here working, and Mikey asked me to bring him something to eat. He's made Conor's favorite soup and I have a thermos full of it under my arm.

The club is empty as I walk to Conor's office. The door is closed and I knock softly and wait to be invited in. A few seconds later, the door opens and I see the room is full of people. There are around twelve men in suits standing and sitting in the room, while Conor sits at his desk. All of them have serious looks on their faces and I realize I've just interrupted an important meeting for clam chowder.

My cheeks flush pink, and I hold up the thermos. "Sorry," I mouth to Conor, who has a fire in his eyes as he glares at me.

"Out! Now!" he barks and I open my mouth in surprise, considering whether to throw this thermos at his head, but then all of the men stand up and start to walk toward the door and I realize he was talking to them and not me. They all nod politely to me as they pass and I watch them with a sudden nervous sensation in the pit of my stomach. The last one to leave closes the door behind himself and I stand there chewing on my lip.

"Come here," Conor orders, but my legs are like jelly and I stand on the spot staring at him instead.

"I'm sorry I interrupted your important meeting," I whisper.

"I said come here!" he barks and I comply like an obedient puppy because bossy Conor makes my insides melt like liquid chocolate.

I walk toward him and place the thermos on his desk, and as soon as I'm within touching distance, he reaches for me and pulls me onto his lap, so I'm straddling him on his office chair.

"Don't ever apologize for coming down here," he growls as he brushes the hair back from my face. "And don't ever knock on my office door again and stand in the doorway like you don't belong here."

My whole body is trembling now, and the heat starts to build in my core. It seems like he's really pissed about something, or is he just really horny? Or both?

"I don't understand. Why can't I knock?" I ask as I stare into his dark eyes.

"Do my brothers knock?" he scowls at me.

"No," I breathe.

"So, why would you have to?" He wraps my hair around his fist and tilts my head back, rubbing his nose up from the base of my throat and along my jawline. He inhales deeply and I moan softly as I experience a rush of slick heat. "You can walk into this office any time you want to, Angel. You never apologize for being anywhere that I am. You got that?" he says as his free hand drops to my hip and he pulls me down further onto him so that his semi hard cock is pressing against my pussy.

"Yes. Conor!" I pant as the heat starts to spread to my thighs and I rock my hips against him.

"Now that you're here, did you just come to bring me a thermos?" he growls before he dips his head again, and this time he runs his tongue from my collarbone, all the way up my throat and onto my face until he reaches my lips, making my entire body shudders with anticipation.

"It's clam chowder," I whisper as his lips hover over mine, taunting me with the promise of a kiss.

"Clam chowder?" He edges his lips closer and the hand on my hip slides between my thighs as he rubs against my clit through my jeans, using the seam of the denim for friction.

"Yes. I brought you dinner. I don't have time for anything else, I'm afraid," I purr, teasing him right back.

He narrows his eyes at me, but there is a wicked glint in them. "You don't have time for me to fuck you, Angel?" he growls as he presses more firmly against my clit and I grind my hips against his hand.

"No. I'm super busy," I groan, brushing my lips over his jaw.

"You're such a bad liar, Jessie." He keeps rubbing. "You interrupted my important meeting so I could make you come, didn't you?"

"Yes," I groan, unable to take his maddening teasing any longer.

He chuckles softly before he peels my tank top off over my head and tosses it over his shoulder. His warm hands snake around to my back and I shiver as he unhooks my bra easily with one hand, and it slides down my arms, allowing my breasts to fall free. He tugs it off impatiently before he bends his head and sucks one of my nipples into his hot mouth and I moan as the rush of wet heat floods my core. He sucks and nibbles on my hard nipples as he reaches down and unzips my jeans. I run my fingers through his hair and moan softly, making him smile against my skin.

Suddenly, he spins his chair around so we are facing his desk and lifts me from his lap, positioning me on his desk directly in front of him. I swallow hard as I stare at him and he has such a wicked look in his eyes that a shiver of nervous excitement skitters up my spine.

"I want you naked. Right now," he growls as he starts to pull off my jeans and I lift my ass so he can wriggle them over my hips. He grabs hold of my panties too and quickly works them down my legs, before removing them with my socks and sneakers.

A few seconds later, I am completely devoid of clothes on his desk and he pushes his chair back slightly and stares at me, making the flush creep over my chest and neck.

"You are so fucking beautiful," he says, rubbing a hand over his jaw. "I should keep you down here with me all night like this. Dripping your cream onto my desk while you wait for me to fuck you."

I chew on my lip as every nerve ending in my body responds to his words and my pussy walls throb in anticipation. "Conor, please?" I pant as I will him to touch me.

"Fuck! I've got so much work to do tonight, Angel," he says with a sigh. The disappointment must show on my face because he winks at me. "I'm going to fuck you real hard first, though."

"Good," I breathe.

"After I eat your delicious pussy," he grins as he pulls my hips toward him and places one hand on my stomach. "Lie back, Angel."

I do as he tells me as he slides his hands down the inside of my thighs until he reaches my ankles and lifts them, planting a foot on each shoulder.

"Conor," I gasp.

His breath dances across on my skin as his face dips between my thighs. "What, Jessie?" he growls.

"What if someone comes in?"

"Nobody except my brothers would dare walk in here without knocking. And if one of them walks in, well they can join me if they like," he chuckles before he peppers soft kisses along the inside of my thighs and I writhe on the desk as I run my fingers through his hair.

"I can smell how wet you are for me," he growls before he buries his face against my pussy, his tongue pressing into my opening as he rubs his nose over my clit.

"Oh, God," I pant as the surge of wet heat rushes between my thighs, making him groan against me.

"You taste so fucking good," he hisses before he licks my pussy from my entrance to my clit before sucking the bud of flesh into his mouth and flicking it with his tongue.

"Conor," I shout as he makes me come quickly, but he doesn't stop even when I pull at his hair. Instead, he adds two fingers and I lift my hips to meet them and his tongue as he works me expertly, and I am completely lost to him.

"For fuck's sake," he snarls, and I look up, wondering what has caused the sudden change in him.

"I'm fucking busy," he shouts toward the door and I realize someone must have knocked, but I was too busy being on the verge of an orgasm to hear.

"The new contractor is here, Boss."

"Tell him to wait, Chester. And if you disturb me again, I'll fire your ass."

"Okay, Boss," Chester replies and Conor looks down at me again as I blush to the roots of my hair.

"Why are you blushing, Angel?" he grins at me. "You think they didn't already know what we'd be doing in here? I couldn't have sent them out of here any quicker if someone set the club on fire."

"I thought you were just pissed at them, or me."

He frowns at me before, wiping his mouth before pulling me from the desk and back onto his lap.

"Your suit will get dirty." I whisper.

"I'll wipe it. Or I'll go change," he says as he brushes my hair with his damp fingers. "Now, why the hell would I be pissed at you, Angel?"

"I don't know," I shrug. "For a second, I thought it was me you were telling to get out."

"Jessie," he says with a soft sigh. "You know I would never…"

"Yes, I do. You just looked so mad when I opened the door."

"Yeah, well. That was business, Angel. Nothing to do with you."

"Is there anything I can help you with?" I run my hands down the lapels of his jacket.

"You already help me more than you realize."

"You're working too hard."

"I'm fine." He shakes his head, his brow furrowed.

"Is there something on your mind?"

He dusts the back of his knuckles across my cheek as he looks into my eyes. "Do you ever wish there was only one of us to have to deal with?"

"One of you?" It's my turn to frown now. "I don't understand what you mean," I stammer.

"Yes, you do. There are four of us. Do you ever wonder what it would be like to just be with one brother?"

I swallow hard. Where the hell is this coming from? "Is this about Shane?"

"It has nothing to do with Shane. It's a simple question, Jessie."

And there it is again, that anger I saw in him earlier. "Of course I don't," I tell him honestly. "Do you wonder about it?"

"About what it would be like to have you to myself? Yes," he admits.

"Oh? Does that mean you're not happy with this arrangement then?" I shift on his lap and he wraps his arms around my waist, holding me tighter to him.

"No!" he says as he stands again and plants me back on the desk. "I love sharing you with my brothers, and I never want that to stop. But of course I think about what it would be like to have you in my bed every single night, Angel, and I'm sure my brothers do too," he growls as he unbuckles his belt before unzipping his suit pants and taking out his cock. It glistens with precum and I lick my lips at the memory of the taste of him. Grabbing onto my hips, he prepares to rail into me, but there is something I want to ask him first.

"How many women have you fucked in this office?"

He tilts his head and frowns at me. "Too many, Angel," he hisses before he drives his cock into me and I moan so loudly, I am sure that all of his employees outside heard me. He leans over me, his face so close to mine that I smell my arousal on him. "But I promise you are going to be the only woman I ever fuck in here ever again. Okay?"

"Okay," I breathe as he drives into me again and nails me to his desk, fucking us both to the release that we so desperately need.

CHAPTER
NINETEEN
JESSIE

I showered as soon as I got back up to the apartment, and dressed suitably for my evening of strip poker with Mikey. As I'm walking to the den to meet him, he saunters up behind me and slaps my ass. "You ready to get your ass whooped, Red?" he chuckles in my ear.

He's dressed in gray sweatpants, and judging by the outline of his huge cock in them, absolutely nothing else. "You're very sure of yourself," I laugh at him. "I'm not that bad at poker, you know?"

He looks me up and down. "Then why are you wearing more clothes than I've ever seen you in before," he says as he pulls the neck of hooded sweatshirt and peers inside, confirming I'm wearing a tank top too.

"I'm cold," I shrug.

"Hmm." He leans close and plants a soft kiss on my neck. "This apartment is boiling, though. I turned up the heat."

"Cheat!" I laugh.

"Says the woman wearing socks!" he laughs. "You have never worn socks in this apartment without your sneakers. Not once."

"Well, I still think your strategy is overly confident," I glance down at his sweatpants.

"Ah, but I got me a secret weapon, Red," he winks at me as he slips his arm around my waist and we walk to the den. "We have ourselves a third player."

"Conor?" I arch an eyebrow at him. "I thought he was working?"

Mikey chuckles as we walk into the den. "Conor is good at poker, but I got the man who taught him everything he knows."

That's when I notice the laptop on the table. "Shane?"

"The one and only," Mikey grins at me.

There is no one on the screen yet, simply an empty hotel room. I strain my eyes to see the bed and whether there is any evidence of Erin being there, but all I see is a perfectly made bed and Shane's cell phone on the nightstand.

"Shane!" Mikey shouts, and a few seconds later Shane fills the screen as he sits on a chair directly in front of his laptop. He's wearing a white shirt and suit pants and he looks so good it makes my pussy contract.

"Evening. We ready to play some poker?" he smiles.

"How exactly are we going to play like this? How do we deal you in?" I ask.

He holds up a pack of playing cards. "I'll deal three hands, just like you're both in the room with me."

"Hmm." I raise an eyebrow at him. "That's very convenient for you."

He places a hand over his heart and winces. "Of all the things you have ever said to me, Jessie, accusing me of cheating at cards has to be the most hurtful," he says with a wicked grin that makes my insides melt and causes Mikey to chuckle.

"Jessie's wearing socks, Shane," Mikey adds.

"Socks?" Shane arches an eyebrow. "Really? And I'm the cheat?"

"I'm cold," I shrug.

"Hmm. Judging by Mikey's attire, it looks freezing there."

"Well, I think Mikey is overconfident, and I am simply prepared," I add as I settle back in my chair.

"Well, we'll see how your strategy plays out, won't we, Hacker? Just so I understand where we're at, how many things you wearing, Mikey?" Shane asks.

"One."

Shane laughs. "You are confident. I'm wearing three."

I do the math in my head. Shirt. Pants. Boxers.

"How about you, Jessie?" Shane growls.

More math. "Seven."

"Cheat!" Mikey grins.

"Mikey!" Shane gently chides him. "If Jessie chooses to wear more clothes tonight, than she usually wears in a week, then that's her choice. I have every confidence she's going to be naked very soon anyway."

"We'll see," I say with a sense of confidence I don't feel because Shane Ryan plays poker like he does everything else in life — to win.

To my complete surprise, I win the first hand. I consider which of them needs to remove some clothes, and there is only one logical choice. I really don't want to be distracted by Mikey's nakedness for the whole evening, and besides that, Shane looks much finer out of his shirt than in it. He removes his shirt with a grumble, but it's only when he sits back down and he and Mikey share a look that I realize I've just been completely played. He wanted to be shirtless. Now he's more comfortable, and I'm even more distracted.

A little over two hours later, I am predictably completely

naked while Shane and Mikey are still in their pants. I didn't win a single hand after the first one.

"For someone with your skills, Hacker, I'm surprised you're not much better at poker?" Mikey grins at me.

"I am good at poker," I protest. "But your brother is a shark! I'm sure he's counting cards there."

"Again with the cheating insults," Shane shakes his head as though he is deeply wounded.

"You had three aces in one of those hands, Shane!" I try to glare at him but I'm too happy to. The truth is, the three of us have had a great time and I haven't seen either Shane or Mikey this relaxed for a long time. Shane has been gone for four days and I haven't spoken to him since the day he left. I was worried things were going to be frosty between us again, but he seems to have forgiven me for turning him down the night we got Liam back from the Russians.

"Luck of the Irish," Shane says with a shrug.

Mikey laughs as he collects up our cards and chips from the table and I pick up my panties from the floor.

"Mikey!" Shane says in that low, gravelly tone that makes me melt, and the atmosphere in the room changes in an instant.

"Yeah?" Mikey looks between Shane and me.

"Can you give us half an hour?" he growls.

"Sure," Mikey says before standing up. He cups my chin in his hand and tilts my head before sealing my mouth with a kiss. "I'll be waiting for you, Red. Don't put any of those damn clothes back on," he growls too.

"I won't," I whisper.

When Mikey has left the room, I focus on the laptop screen, biting my lip in anticipation.

"Go sit on the sofa, Jessie, and put the laptop on the coffee table in front of you."

I could ask why. I could remind him that we don't do this

kind of stuff anymore. But, I am hot, and wet, and I miss him so much. Besides, he can't actually touch me, can he? So, no matter what we do now, we're not breaking any of our rules.

Picking up the computer, I do as Shane asks and sit down on the sofa, placing the laptop directly in front of me.

"Now, lean back and put your feet on the table. One on either side of the screen," he commands.

I blush at the thought of his view from the other side of the camera if I do that. "Shane!"

"It's nothing I haven't seen before, sweetheart."

"I get that. But..."

"I won, right? And this is the prize I choose. Feet up, Jessie. Now! I want to see that beautiful pink pussy."

The heat floods my body as I do as he orders and place my feet on the table, so I am completely spread open for him.

"Fuck! Your cunt is beautiful."

The wet heat rushes between my thighs at his words. "What now?" I breathe.

"Now, I want to watch you while you make yourself come."

I suck in a breath and he groans softly. "Do you ever think about me when you touch yourself, Jessie?"

"Yes," I admit.

"Good. Because I've already jerked off twice today thinking about you. Now show me how you touch yourself when you're thinking about me, Hacker."

He thinks about me! "I can't." I bite my lip and shake my head. I'm too self-conscious.

"Jessie!" he growls loudly as he unzips his fly and pulls his cock out of his suit pants. Even from here, I can see it is rock hard and glistening with precum, and my body trembles at the memory of him inside me. "If I was there with you, I'd be burying my cock in your cunt right now."

"Shane," I groan loudly because I love his filthy mouth.

"I can see already you're soaking, Hacker. You know that you want this as much as I do. Now slide your hand down to that beautiful, wet cunt and touch yourself for me."

I slide my hand down my body, between my thighs, until I find my already swollen clit. My fingers glide easily over the slick bud and I bite my lip to stifle a groan before I close my eyes and tilt my head back.

"Eyes on me, Hacker. You don't get to come for me if you're not looking at me."

I lift my head and open my eyes, watching as he strokes his cock while he glares at my pussy and my fingers working.

"And stop biting your damn lip. I want to hear every sound you make," he growls as the pace of his own stroking increases.

"You're so damn bossy," I groan as the tremors of pleasure build in my abdomen and thighs.

"You'd better believe it, Hacker. Fuck! I wish I was there right now. I'd slip two fingers inside you and make you squeeze me tight. You remember how it feels when I fuck you with my fingers?"

"Yes," I pant, as a rush of wet heat almost makes me lose control.

"Slip two fingers inside yourself then, sweetheart. And pretend they're mine. Tell me how good your cunt feels."

"Shane," I pant as I watch him gripping his cock while he talks filthy to me. But I glide my other hand between my thighs and push two fingers inside and arch my back in pleasure.

"How does that feel, Jessie?" he groans.

"So good," I breathe. "But I wish it was you," I say, entirely lost in the moment and forgetting that we told each other we couldn't do this anymore. But this isn't real, is it? He's not actually touching me.

"I wish it was me too, sweetheart. Being inside your cunt is my fucking nirvana. Now, tell me how wet you are," he hisses, and I can tell he is on the edge.

"I'm soaking for you, Shane," I moan as I grind down onto my fingers while I increase the pressure on my clit. "You make me come so hard."

"Fuck! Jessie!" he roars and watching him spurt his seed onto his own hand as he loses control is so damn hot that it tips me over the edge too and my climax washes over me in long rolling waves as I continue rubbing out the last tremors of pleasure from my body. I straighten up when I'm done, my cheeks flushed pink and panting for breath. I smile at him.

"Dammit, Jessie. I'm gonna have to get these pants dry cleaned," he laughs softly.

"I think we might need to steam clean the sofa too," I glance between my thighs before I arch an eyebrow at him.

"Have you got cum on the sofa, sweetheart?" he growls, and the heat floods through me again.

"A little," I breathe.

"Fuck. You make me so fucking hard, Jessie. I miss you."

"I miss you too, Shane," I whisper and then we just stare at each other through the screen, neither of us saying any of the things we do desperately need to. "When will you be home?" I finally ask when I can bear the tension no longer.

"A few days," he says and the change in his tone is evident. He looks away from the screen and zips up his fly. "I have to go," he snaps.

I swallow the emotion down at the sudden coolness in him. He is annoyed at himself because he has let his guard down with me. But he instigated this. Not me. "Okay," I stand up and pick up the laptop to switch it off. "I guess I'll see you in a few days."

"Jessie!" he says as I'm about to disconnect.

"What, Shane?"

He licks his lip and stares at me for a few seconds before he speaks. "When you're being fucked by my brother in a few minutes, remember that it was me who made you soaking wet for him."

"You're an arrogant asshole, you know that?" I shake my head, but I can't help but smile at him.

"I do, but you love it, right?"

"Goodnight, Shane," I reply before I close the lid and end the call.

TWENTY

MIKEY

As I sit on the edge of Liam's bed, I smile as I watch my sleeping twin. I woke him to see if he needed anything and he rolled over and told me to go to hell, so that is a sure sign he's getting better. The meds he's on are some heavy duty shit and they make him sleep sixteen hours a day. I fucking miss him. I miss him being at my side when we're doing anything, but especially when we're working, and with Shane away, me and Conor are working even harder than ever. But I know that this is what he needs and I would let him sleep for a whole fucking year if it means getting him back to the way he was before.

I've grown up with all three of my brothers always looking out for me. Apart from the occasional disagreement and the general busting each other's balls that comes with being a sibling, we rarely fight or argue. I would die for any one of them and I believe without a doubt that they would do the same for me.

Listening to Vlad talking to Jessie today about her father and uncle made me appreciate that I sometimes take their unwavering loyalty and love for granted. There is nothing any of them could do that would make me betray them, or Jessie. She has fit into our tight family unit so seamlessly and perfectly that I wonder how we lived without her. I fucking adore her, and my brothers do too. The fact that we are able to share her without any egos or jealousy getting in the way is a testament to our bond. Each of us ultimately wants what is best for the others, and that's why we operate as such an efficient unit. So when Shane asked for some time alone with her, there was no question that I would step back and give him that. He's out there alone on the road, and he needed her more than me. And she needed him too. Although she does her best to hide it, I see the pain in her eyes whenever his name is mentioned, and I hope they sort their shit out because they are so much better together.

The sound of Liam groaning in his sleep breaks my train of thought. "Jessie," he says in a way that I've heard him say plenty of times before, usually when the two of us are deep inside her. I can't help but laugh, pleased that he is having such pleasant dreams, but I think that's my cue to leave. Besides, it's been a while since I left Jessie and Shane alone, and I hope to be inside her for real very soon. That thought makes my cock twitch to life. I have never enjoyed fucking any woman quite so much as my Red.

I LIE in her bed waiting for her and smile when I hear her soft footsteps outside the open door. She pops her head inside. "Did you check on Liam?"

"Yeah. He's sleeping like a baby. So get your ass in here."

She laughs softly before she steps into the room, not bothering to close the door in case Liam shouts for one of us, and also because both he and Conor have watched us fuck plenty of times so neither she, or I, care if they were to wander in. My eyes roam over her sexy little body. "Why the hell are you wearing panties, Red?" I growl when I see them.

"I just put them on in case I had to go check on Liam is all," she bites her lip and blushes.

I sit up in bed. "Get over here. Now!"

She walks over to me, still chewing her lip and trying to look all innocent when she has a body that must have been hand carved by the devil himself, because every single part of it screams *sin*. As soon as she's within touching distance, I reach up and pull her down onto the bed, making her squeal as I roll on top of her. "I told you not to put any of those clothes back on," I growl before I brush my lips over her breasts.

"I just..." She doesn't finish the sentence, instead she moans loudly as I suck a nipple into my mouth and bite. "Mikey!" she gasps and every drop of blood in my body feels like it rushes straight to my cock.

"Would you disobey Shane or Conor like that?" I growl before kissing a trail to her other breast.

"Maybe. Depending on what mood I'm in," she giggles before I bite on her other nipple and she arches her back in pleasure until she's grinding herself onto my cock.

"What am I going to do with you, Red?" I chuckle softly as I trail kisses down her stomach until I reach the waistband of her panties. I kiss her mound through them and she moans softly. "Please, Mikey?"

"If only these panties weren't in my way, I could eat your sweet pussy right now," I growl as I move lower, kissing her folds through the damp black fabric. She smells fucking delicious and I am desperate to taste her, but I love to make her beg.

"Take them off," she groans as her hands fumble at the waistband, but she can't remove them because my face is pressed up against her pussy. "Please?"

"But if you wanted them off, why did you put them back on

when I specifically told you not to, Jessie?" I keep kissing her and her hands move to my head instead, running her fingers through my hair. "Don't you want to be fucked tonight?"

"You know I do," she groans. "I'm sorry, Mikey. I need you. Please?"

I can't resist the sound of her pleading for me, and I tug her panties to one side and slide a finger through her wet folds. "Damn, Jessie. What did Shane just do to you? You're fucking soaking," I smile as I push a finger inside her hot wet pussy and she groans so loudly I think she might have woken Liam at the other end of the hall. "Is that what you need, Red?"

"Yes," she hisses as I push deeper inside her and she grinds herself on my finger. I add two more at once, stretching her wider and making her gasp out loud. Her walls squeeze me tight, drawing me in deeper as her sweet fucking juices run down my fingers and onto my wrist as I work her. "Oh, Red, you're desperate for it, aren't you?" I groan. "You're such a bad girl spreading your legs for my brother and then coming in here looking to be fucked."

"Mikey. Please?" she moans again, and the sound makes my cock feel like it's about to burst. The smell of her wet heat is driving me fucking crazy and as much as I enjoy teasing her and making her beg, I can't hold out much longer. I bend my head low and suck her sweet little bud into my mouth and damn if she isn't the sweetest thing I have ever tasted in my life.

As I nudge her clit with my tongue, I push my fingers deeper and she rewards me with an orgasm that vibrates through her entire body. Her fingers in my hair, her juices in my mouth and all over my hand, make my balls draw up into my stomach. I push myself up while she's still shuddering and pull my fingers out of her, pushing my sweatpants off quickly to allow my poor weeping cock free. Reaching down, I rip the damn panties off her, tearing the fabric down the middle because I am fucking frantic to be inside her.

"The next time I tell you not to put your panties back on," I growl as I take her hands and pin them down onto the bed on either side of her head and line my cock up against her slick entrance. "You will do as you are fucking told."

"Okay," she pants as she looks up at me and then I watch those beautiful blue eyes almost roll out of the back of her head as I drive my cock deep inside her. I want to be the only man inside her right now — her pussy and her head.

"Who just made you come, Jessie?"

"You did," she groans as she wraps her legs around my waist and raises her hips up to meet mine, pulling me deeper inside her.

I fuck her hard and the room is filled with her moaning and the slick, wet sound of my cock filling her dripping pussy.

Fuck, my girl loves being dominated in bed. "You love being fucked, don't you, Red?" I whisper in her ear before grazing my teeth over the soft, sweet smelling skin on her neck. I am about to lose my fucking mind buried inside this woman. She drives me fucking crazy.

"Yes," she moans softly and her pussy squeezes me tighter. "Mikey," she half shouts, half moans, and I swear there is no better sound than my name on her lips when she comes. I bury my face in her neck, nailing her to the bed as I grind out the last of her orgasm while her body shudders beneath me before finally finding my own.

When we're both done, I lie there, my cock still inside her and my forehead pressed against hers.

"I like your bossy side," she purrs like a kitten.

"Yeah, I kinda got that, Red," I chuckle.

"I'm sorry for wearing panties."

"If I had my way, you'd never wear panties again."

"Well, that could be a little inconvenient, and very distracting," she giggles. "Especially around you and your brothers. I'm not sure any of us would ever get any work done."

"Hmm. You're probably right, Red. Which is why it's also probably a good thing that I don't get to make the rules around here."

"Probably," she agrees as I pull out of her and roll off her, pulling her with me until she is curled up against my chest with her thigh resting on mine and our cum dripping onto my leg, but I don't give a damn about that right now. All I want is to lie here with her, holding her close.

"You think we should get cleaned up?" she suggests.

"No point," I say, stifling an unexpected yawn. "I'm not done with you yet. I plan on getting you dirty again very soon."

"Really? It seems like you should get some sleep. You've been working so hard. I'll still be here in the morning."

"I'll sleep when I'm dead, Red. It has been so fucking long since I spent the night with you. And that's fine because Liam has needed you, but know that tonight, you are going to be fucked repeatedly. Your mouth. Your pussy, and your juicy ass." I squeeze it and she shivers. "So much that you're going to be hobbling around this apartment all day tomorrow."

"Sounds attractive," she giggles as she snuggles closer to me. "I'll just spend the day in bed watching movies with Liam."

"I wish I could join you," I groan.

She lifts her head and looks down at me with concern on her face. "Is there something I can do to help? You and Conor are working so hard, and I'm just in the apartment doing nothing most of the time."

Fuck me this woman is beautiful inside and out. "No. You make our food. You do our laundry. You keep us company when we need it. You let us fuck you whenever we feel like." That last part is kind of a joke even though it's true, and she opens her mouth to respond but I brush my fingers over her cheek. "And most importantly, you take care of Liam. He needs you, Red. And I know without a doubt, that he wouldn't be doing as well as he is if you weren't by his side every day. So, no, there is absolutely nothing more you can do."

"Okay," she sighs softly and rests her head on my chest again.

"Besides, Shane will be back soon, and things can get back to normal round here."

"Yeah," she says, but there is a sadness in her at the mention of his name.

"You two will be okay, you know?" I was worried that he wouldn't let her in again, but I don't see how that's possible. I see the way he looks at her. He loves her as much as he always has, and she is pretty impossible not to like, or forgive. And after whatever just happened in the den, he must be coming around because he wouldn't play with her heart like that.

"I hope so," she whispers.

TWENTY-ONE

SHANE

I slip on my Ray Bans as I walk down the airplane steps and into the glaring LA sunshine. A car waits for me at the bottom and a driver opens the door as I approach.

"Good afternoon, Mr Ryan." He bows his head slightly.

"Afternoon," I reply with a nod before he opens the door wider and I bend my head and climb inside, surprised to see a figure sitting waiting for me.

"Hola, amigo," Alejandro Montoya smiles widely at me.

"What the hell?" I grin back at him as I sit on opposite end of the back seat. "When you said you were sending a car for me, I didn't realize you'd be in it."

"Well, there's been a change of plans," he says with a shake of his head. "Jax has had to go out of town and I have some business I need to deal with this afternoon. Then I have to go to some charity thing with Alana later. It's a last minute deal, but it's important to my wife, so I'm sorry, amigo, our planned night of drunken debauchery will have to wait. But I have booked you into the best suite at my hotel and everything you indulge in there is on the house."

"Thank you. And I'm not sure you calling off our night out is a bad thing," I laugh. "I have a meeting at 8am."

He laughs too. "Well, my ideas of debauchery these days are much tamer anyway. I am a one-woman man. You'd probably think I'm boring now."

"I'm not sure you could ever be considered boring, Alejandro," I grin at him. "Besides, I see the appeal."

"You do, huh?" He flashes an eyebrow at me. "Is this the computer hacker?"

"It's complicated," I shake my head. "Far too complicated to explain during a drive to the city anyway." Thinking about Jessie gives me a pain in my chest. Last night was supposed to just be a game of poker. Strip poker, granted, but just a friendly game. Mikey had asked me to help get Jessie naked, and that was all I intended to do. But I obviously forgot what seeing her naked body does to me. And then when I watched her on that computer making herself come for me, I was tempted to catch the next flight home and fuck her for real. The memory of her smell and the taste of her, of how her cunt squeezes my cock, overwhelm me whenever I think of her. But, I can deal with those. It's the memory of how it feels to be loved by her that I can't handle.

Alejandro stares at me intently and I realize I'm completely lost in thoughts of her once more. "Women, my friend. Our reason for living and the reason our hair turns gray," he winks at me before holding up a bottle of Jameson and I nod before he pours us each a glass.

"So, you were asking about this Wolf guy?" Alejandro says as he hands me my drink and settles back against his seat, and I'm thankful for the distraction.

"Yeah. You ever had any dealings with him at all?"

"No." Alejandro shakes his head. "But he was Russian, right? I don't exactly get on with the Bratva, Shane."

"You never used to get on with the Irish either," I remind him. Before my brothers and I took over, a man named Seamus Finnan ran operations, and Alejandro almost sawed off his head with a steak knife during one particular showdown in a New York restaurant.

"Well, that was in my younger and more reckless days," he says with a chuckle. "Besides, Seamus was a prick. And you're not. I trust you."

"Well, you helped my brothers and me out a lot when we first came to the States. We've always got your back."

"And I yours, amigo," he says before knocking back his whiskey.

"So, you know nothing about him then?" I ask again. If I didn't know that he existed, I would think the Wolf was a figment of someone's imagination, he is that fucking elusive.

"Only what everyone else knows. The Bratva's top assassin. Disappeared ten years ago after he slaughtered that family and kidnapped your girl."

My girl. Dammit Jessie!

"I even had Jax do a little digging for you but he came up with nothing."

I shake my head in frustration. Jax is the human equivalent of a bloodhound. The fact that neither he nor Jessie can find the Wolf gives me little hope that we will ever find him unless he wants to be found. And I can't help that worry her being with me and my brothers makes her more visible to him.

"You worried he's still out there and he might come after her again?" Alejandro asks, as if reading my thoughts.

"Yep. And if I don't know who he is, then how the fuck do I protect her from him? I worry about her every time she leaves the apartment. I worry that he's so fucking invisible he might walk right past me one day and take her from under my nose."

"You do what you can, Shane. That's all any of us can do. I

used to worry about Alana too. Fuck, I still do. And I had reason to after what happened to her. But, trying to second-guess everything and everyone, trying to keep her in a cage, well it drove both of us crazy."

"So, how do you deal with it?"

He sucks in a deep breath. "I choose not to let it overwhelm me. Now that we have the kids too, I could worry about all of them all day long, so I have to consciously make an effort not to. She and the boys never leave the house without a bodyguard, and I trust that she does everything she can to keep herself and our children safe."

"And Lucia?" I ask, referring to his adopted adult daughter.

"Don't even," he says with a shake of his head. "That girl can take care of herself and I swear she is even more stubborn than both me and Alana combined, so I let her do her own thing. I have given up trying to give myself an aneurysm arguing with the kid."

I smile at the image that conjures in my head. Alejandro Montoya is one of the fiercest and most ruthless men I've ever met, but he is completely besotted with his wife and children, and there is a distinct change in him when he talks about them. I finish my whiskey and lean back in my seat.

"We chose this life, Shane. We don't get to make the people who love us suffer for it too. So, we do what we can to keep them safe and then we let them do what makes them happy."

"I suppose so."

"Damn. I've never seen you like this over a woman," he laughs.

"Like what?"

He doesn't reply, simply shakes his head before he pours us each another drink.

"I hate it," I admit. "I wish I could stop thinking about her."

"She doesn't feel the same?" he frowns at me.

"She does. At least I think she does."

"Ah, love," he says with a sigh. "It's an incredible thing — even when it hurts like hell."

"So, what's this business you have to deal with?" I ask him, desperate to change the subject.

He flashes his eyebrows at me. "Why? You in that much need for a distraction? You want in?"

"Does it involve breaking bones?"

"It can," he answers with a grin.

"Then I'm in."

"Great. Maybe with your help I won't have to get blood on my best suit," he says before pouring us each another drink.

THE WHISKEY BURNS my throat as I swallow a huge mouthful. Staring out at the LA skyline as I roll the glass in my hand, I wonder what my brothers and Jessie are doing back home. Mostly I wonder about her. What she is wearing. Whether she is happy or sad. Whether she is thinking about me. With a shake of my head, I put the glass onto the table and sit on the sofa. I've drunk too much tonight and it's making me far too reflective and melancholy for my own good. Even breaking some faces with Alejandro today wasn't enough of a distraction. Sitting here alone in my hotel room night after night isn't helping either. I should be down in the bar. I haven't had sex for three long months and I have never gone this long without fucking before. The last time was with Jessie when we kept her a prisoner in our basement. The memory of that day makes my cock stiffen in my pants. Damn, that woman gets under my skin like no one I have ever known.

The women in LA are hot, and the women who stay in Alejandro's hotels are rich and hot, which means they take good care of themselves. I shake my head, pissed at myself for even thinking about it. So, clearly I'm not that wasted because I know that is a line I can't even think about crossing. Not until I've figured out what the hell is going on with Jessie and me.

As I glance at the table, I see my cell phone sitting there, daring me to call her and tell her that I can't stop thinking about her. I pick it up and dial Conor instead. It rings and rings, but he doesn't answer. It's after midnight in New York so he's probably working in the club, so it's not that unusual that he doesn't pick up, but it still sets my nerves on edge not to be able to speak to him. I end the call without leaving a message and dial Mikey instead, who picks up on the fourth ring.

"Hey, bro? How are things in sunny LA?" he asks.

"Boring as fuck."

"Oh," he laughs softly.

"Where is Conor? I can't get a hold of him?"

"Well, he caught one of the new bar staff skimming money from the cash register so he's enjoying firing his ass in true Conor style as we speak."

"Ouch," I wince at the thought of what the bartender is currently being subjected to. Not that the piece of shit doesn't deserve it. You have to be a special kind of stupid to steal money from our club right under our noses. "How is Liam doing?"

"Great. He's sleeping loads still, but the doc says that's a good thing to let his body heal. He should be back on his feet in a day or so. He can hobble to the bathroom on his own now, so that's good. And when he's awake, he's good. Jessie spends most of the day with him, playing cards and watching TV. So the lazy fucker is living his best life really," Mikey jokes, but I know that no one is more relieved than he is that Liam is okay.

"Glad to hear it. And you?"

"Tired. But all good, bro. Looking forward to you coming home though. It's not the same without you."

"I'm looking forward to coming home too," I tell him, and

then we're silent for a few moments until I'm forced to speak again, if only to break the tension that has edged into what was supposed to be a lighthearted catch up with the brother who is the least likely of all of us to talk about feelings with me. "How is she?" I swallow the ball of emotion that is lodged in my throat.

"Ask her yourself, bro," he sighs.

"But I'm asking you, Mikey," I snap, and then I feel bad for taking my frustration out on him. "I mean after yesterday. Is she okay?"

"Why? What did you two do? Because she was pretty happy, and dripping wet, by the time she came to bed."

"You're welcome," I smile and can't help experiencing a sense of perverted satisfaction and pride at what he just told me. "But I meant after what happened with Vlad."

"Ask her yourself," he repeats. "I told you what went down yesterday at the park. And I'm not getting any more involved than that."

"You're an asshole."

"And it sounds like you've had too much to drink. So, get some sleep and I'll talk to you tomorrow."

"Are you really trying to be the responsible one here?"

"Well, one of us has to be, Shane. Because you are losing your edge," he replies, and I can't tell if he is joking or being truthful, or maybe a little of both. I end the call without saying anything else and let him go back to whatever he was doing before I disturbed him. Scrolling through my contacts, I pause at her name, my finger hovering over the call button. She is probably asleep. But what the hell? I dial her number anyway.

After a few rings, she answers. "Hi. What's up?" she asks quietly and sleepily.

"Did I wake you?"

"Yes. But it's okay. Is something wrong?" she whispers.

"Why are you whispering?"

"Because Liam is sleeping. Hold on, let me go into the den," she says and I hear her soft breathing as she climbs out of bed and walks to the other room. "There. I can talk now," she says louder now. "Are you okay?"

"No," I admit in a drunken moment of weakness.

I hear the breath catch in her throat. "Why? Has something happened? Shane?" her voice goes up a few octaves too and the concern in it gives me a perverse sense of satisfaction. Not that I needed proof that she cares for me. Despite everything that has happened between us, I do believe that.

"I'm fine," I lie now, not wanting to cause her any distress when she is thousands of miles away.

"Have you been drinking?"

"Yes!" *Fuck! Do I really sound that drunk?*

"Do you need something?" she asks, and I can't tell whether it is frustration or something else creeping into her voice.

"Yes." *You.*

"What is it, Shane?" she says, softer now.

I love you, Jessie Ryan. "I'm think I'm homesick, is all."

"Homesick?" she laughs softly. "Then come home."

"I have a meeting tomorrow. And then…" I trail off. "I'll be home in a few days."

"I wish I could do something to make you feel better."

"You already have." I say that out loud, even though I only meant to think it. "Night, Jessie."

"Night, Shane."

I throw my phone onto the sofa beside me, and I lean back before closing my eyes. Was Mikey right about me losing my edge? Maybe I need to cancel my meeting in Vegas the day after tomorrow? Maybe I need to get my ass back on a plane to New York.

TWENTY-TWO

Liam has an arm wrapped around my shoulder as he shuffles back to bed from the bathroom. He's much more mobile now and insists on doing everything himself as much as possible. But this morning, he attempted a shower for the first time on his own and I found him sitting on the plastic chair Mikey put in the stall for him with the water shut off and him struggling to get back up.

"You should have waited for me," I admonish him. "You could have really hurt yourself."

"It was only a shower, Jessie. I wasn't trying to run a marathon," he snaps at me, his frustration at his body not being able to do everything he wants it to clearly evident, and I am reminded how difficult this must be for him. I understand how frustrating it is to need to push your body to do more than it is physically capable of. When I was first kidnapped by the Wolf, I was a weak little girl. By the time I escaped almost two years later, I was a strong woman capable of so much more than he ever gave me credit for.

"Sorry," he sighs as we reach the bed and he sits down on it. "I thought I'd be able to do it on my own."

"And you will be soon. But you've only been back on your feet for two days, Liam. You're doing incredible, but if you push too hard, you'll set yourself back."

He rolls his eyes and lies back on the bed.

"Now stop making me nag you. I feel like I'm your mother," I say as I jump on the bed beside him, leaning on my elbow as I look at his bruised face.

"Trust me, Jessie, there is nothing at all that is motherly about you," he chuckles softly.

I open my mouth in shock, about to reprimand him after the way I have looked after him.

"At least not to me," he adds quickly as he holds a hand up in surrender. "But you are the hottest damn nurse I've ever seen."

"Good save." I narrow my eyes at him as I place my hand lightly on his chest.

"Come here," he whispers, holding up his index finger and beckoning me closer.

I lean my face closer to his. "Here?"

He shakes his head and traces his fingertip over his lips. "Here."

I edge closer, pressing my lips softly against his and kissing him. He slides his tongue into my mouth and our kiss becomes something much more. The familiar heat builds in my core and I pull back from him, sucking in a breath as I stare into his dark eyes.

"Jessie," he groans.

"You need to take it easy, sunshine."

He reaches up, his injured fingers curling gently in my hair. "I've had enough taking it easy. I need you."

I shake my head. "We can't. You're still recovering."

"This is part of my recovery. We need to check all my parts

are still working right," he glances down, and I look too, to see his thick cock standing to attention.

"He looks like he's working just fine to me." I arch an eyebrow at him. "So why don't I go make you something to eat and you can let him calm down?"

"The only thing I want to eat is your pussy," he growls, pulling me back to him and pressing my lips to his as he kisses me, full of fire and need and longing.

He needs air before I do, and he breaks our kiss first. "Please, Jessie. I really need you."

"And I need you too. But I will never forgive myself if hurt you. And then it will take you even longer to recover, and everyone will be super pissed at me. And we'll have to wait even longer to do this."

He shakes his head. "You won't hurt me. Slide yourself onto my cock, baby." He runs a hand down my back and beneath my t-shirt and I shiver from his touch. I miss him too. I would love to do just that, but I meant what I said.

"I'll hurt you," I say with a shake of my head.

"You're my nurse, right?" He flashes his eyebrows at me.

"I suppose." I chew on my lip.

"Well, nurse Jessie. Your patient is in severe pain right now, because all of the blood that he needs for his vital organs is currently rushing straight to his cock. And that," he nods toward it, "is fucking painful, baby."

"I am not riding you like a rodeo bull while you have broken ribs," I say as I push myself up.

He frowns at me.

"But," I go on as I start to trail kisses down his chest and over his perfectly chiseled abs. "I will do something about this if it makes you feel more comfortable."

"Jessie," he groans as his fingers run softly through my hair. "I'd prefer your pussy, baby. But I suppose your mouth will do."

"You suppose?" I murmur against his skin and he chuckles softly.

I move lower, peppering his fresh, soapy smelling skin with soft kisses until I reach his cock. I place a kiss on the base of his shaft and it twitches, making him groan loudly. I smile as I move past it, down toward his thighs and his balls, trailing butterfly kisses over his skin.

"Jessie," he growls now as his fingers tighten their grip.

"Liam," I breathe against him as I move my head and lightly lick the precum from the tip of his shaft.

"Jessie! Please!" he hisses and I can't help but chuckle.

"So, that's what that feels like," I purr softly against his skin.

"What?" he gasps as I cup his balls in my hand and squeeze lightly as I lick his length from root to tip.

"Well, it's usually me begging one of you guys, isn't it? Not the other way around. I quite like it."

"I never make you beg, baby. I always give you what you need," he groans.

"Hmm," I say as I continue teasing him with soft kisses and just the tip of my tongue.

"Fuck!" he hisses, and I smile.

"Tell me what you need, baby," I tease him.

"Suck my cock. Now!" he growls and the wet heat sears between my thighs as I suck his beautiful cock into my mouth, taking him all the way to the back of my throat and the groans of pleasure rumble through his body. I suck him, running the flat of my tongue along the underside of his shaft before swirling it over the tip and starting again.

"Damn! Jessie. Where the hell did you learn to suck cock like that, baby?" he hisses, as he rocks his hips into my mouth. "Fuck!" he growls a few moments later as he comes in my mouth and I swallow it greedily before sucking and licking him clean. When I lift my head, he is looking down at me, his eyes dark with desire and lust.

"You feel better now?" I say as I wipe my mouth and move back up the bed.

"Uh-huh," he grunts his response before his head falls flat against the pillow.

"That good?" I grin at him.

"I wish I could return the favor, baby," he says with a sigh.

"Oh, I'll make sure that you do as soon as you're able to. Don't worry." I wink at him and am rewarded with one of his amazing smiles — the kind that makes his eyes twinkle and crinkle at the corners.

"I love you so fucking much."

"I love you too, handsome." I kiss his lips softly. "Now, I'm going to make you something to eat so you can take your meds. Do not move from this bed while I'm out of the room."

"I won't, Boss."

TWENTY-THREE

JESSIE

Dropping the weight onto the floor, I stand up and flex my shoulders. I glance up at Conor and Mikey finishing their pull-ups and stare unashamedly at their glistening bodies as their muscles flex and vibrate. Damn, these boys are fine! They have been working so much lately, they haven't been able to fit as many gym sessions in, so I was very happy to see them stroll in halfway through mine this morning. It certainly makes pounding the treadmill more enjoyable when I have such a beautiful view.

"You going to stand there and stare at them all day, or you going to do a bit of work?" Liam chuckles in my ear as he comes up behind me.

"Actually, I've finished my workout." I turn around and wrap my arms around him. "What are you doing in here?"

"Doc said I'm okay for very light cardio," he shrugs. "Thought I'd have a very slow walk on the treadmill?"

"You want company? I can stay?" I offer.

"I'll be fine, baby," he slides his hand to my ass. "But some company later would be good?" he grins at me.

"Light cardio." I arch an eyebrow at him.

"We can watch a movie and fool around. That's light," he chuckles and the wicked glint in his eye makes me experience an overwhelming a rush of love for him.

"You can't. You promised Mikey that you'd finish watching that God-awful TV series with him tonight before he goes to work."

"Shit, yeah. And Cobra Kai isn't awful. It's fucking epic!"

"Whatever you say, handsome." I grin at him. "Enjoy your workout. And don't do too much."

Conor and Liam are between sets and walk over to us. "We'll keep an eye on him, Boss," Mikey says with a wink.

"Make sure that you do!" I lean over and give him and Conor a brief kiss on the cheek before I leave the gym.

As I'm walking down the hallway, I hear the ping of the elevator doors opening and I stop in my tracks. There is only one other person who has access to this apartment, but he's not due back until tomorrow. My heart flutters in anticipation at the prospect of seeing him. I have missed him so much. I wonder if he remembers much of his drunken phone call to me the night before last. I got the impression he wanted to talk about something but he was holding back, as he often does.

He steps out of the elevator and turns straight toward me. As usual, he looks good enough to lick from head to toe, while I must seem like a hot, sweaty mess after my workout. Our eyes lock and I swallow hard as my pulse starts to race. Every single nerve ending in my body is aware of his presence. Goosebumps prickle along my forearms, and I literally stop breathing. He drops his bags onto the floor and walks toward me, and I just stand here staring at him like an idiot until he's standing right in front of me. He glares at me with his beautiful green eyes, and I draw in a breath.

"You brothers are in the gym," I stammer.

"They all okay?"

"Yes." *Just breathe, Jessie!*

"Good. I'll catch up with them later. You okay?"

Apart from feeling like I'm about to pass out or melt into a puddle? "Yes."

He takes one step closer, until our bodies are mere inches apart and I can feel the heat from his body and smell that goddamn intoxicating cologne he wears. As he looks into my eyes, my pulse starts to thrum against all of my pressure points and the heat sears between my thighs. I swear this man can see inside my soul.

A few seconds pass before he slides his hands over my hips and onto my ass and pulls me against him and my entire, traitorous body trembles at his touch. He dips his head, leaning his face close to mine. His breath dances over my cheek and sends a shiver skittering down my spine. "I missed you, Hacker."

"I missed you too, Shane," I whisper.

With no further warning, he lifts me and wraps my legs around his waist, making me gasp, before he begins walking down the hallway. "Shane. Where are you taking me?"

"To bed, sweetheart. It has been way too long since I fucked you."

Damn! I love his filthy mouth. I love everything about him. "But... you and me. We don't..."

"Stop! Talking!" he orders, narrowing his eyes at me before he seals his lips over mine and silences me with a kiss. I melt into him as he literally tongue fucks my mouth, and I whimper shamelessly as I grind my hips against his cock. The waves of pleasure roll through my body as he hardens against my throbbing pussy.

I can barely think straight by the time he walks us into his bedroom and kicks the door closed behind us. Making his way straight to the bed, he throws me onto it and starts taking off his clothes. I can do nothing but stare up at him and watch the spectacle that is Shane Ryan undressing because he has the body of a Greek god. I lick my lips as I think about running my hands over every inch of it very shortly. Because maybe I was wrong? Perhaps just sex with him is better than nothing?

He pushes his jeans and boxers down over his thick, tattooed thighs and when he stands straight again, his beautiful cock is standing to attention.

His eyes are full of fire as he walks over to the bed and crawls over me. He sits back, straddling me with his knees on either side of my hips, and I shiver in anticipation.

"Just so we're clear," he growls as he reaches down and pulls my tank top up before dipping his head low and planting soft kisses over my stomach. "You own every single part of me, Jessie Ryan, and you always have. I am completely and undeniably yours. But I'm done talking, sweetheart. We always seem to screw everything up when we talk. So, I just want to fuck you until the sun comes up tomorrow. Okay?"

The heat sears through my body as wetness pools between my thighs. "Yes," I groan as he pulls my sports bra up and over my head and tosses it onto the floor. He sucks one of my hard nipples into his mouth and nips me gently as he lifts his hips and begins to tug down my yoga pants. I moan loudly when his fingers slide through my slick heat and straight to my dripping pussy.

"So fucking wet," he mumbles against me as he moves lower, trailing kisses over my hot skin. "I need to taste you."

I pull his head away from me as he starts to work my pants off down my legs and I remember that I have spent over an hour in the gym this morning. "Shane, don't," I gasp.

He looks up at me with a scowl on his face. "Why the fuck not?"

"I just worked out. I should take a shower first." I say as the blush creeps over my cheeks.

"Have you got any of my brother's cum in you right now?"

"No." My blush deepens.

He pulls my pants off my legs, along with my socks and sneakers, and throws them across the room. "Then why would I give a fuck that you just worked out, sweetheart? I've already had my tongue in every part of you, and I am desperate to taste you." He dips his head low and runs his tongue along my pussy as if to prove his point, and the loud, animal-like growl that rumbles in his throat makes me giggle.

He looks up and winks at me. "Fucking delicious. Now what did I tell you about not talking," he says as he wraps his arms around the back of my thighs and lies down on the bed like a sniper as he pulls me down towards him until my pussy is practically pressed against his face. "The only words I want to hear from you are, 'oh. God. Fuck. Me. Shane.' Any combination, in any order will do fine," he winks at me again before his head disappears between my thighs and he swirls his tongue over my clit before moving lower and pushing it inside me.

"Oh, fuck! Shane!" I groan loudly as the warmth rolls through my abdomen.

"Good girl." He lifts his head and chuckles, and the sound vibrates through my whole body.

His warm breath skitters over my skin and I squirm as he starts to tease me, peppering the top of my thighs with kisses and tiny delicious bites. "Please, Shane?" I whimper shamelessly.

"Damn! I love how you say my name, Hacker," he growls against me. His kisses move closer to right where I want him until he seals his mouth over my clit again, grazing it gently with his teeth and making my hips jolt off the bed as I feel a rush of wet heat. He presses the flat of his tongue against it and sucks softly, sending endorphins charging around my body.

Every hair on my head tingles with electricity and my thighs tremble as he grips them tighter and holds me tighter to him.

"Oh, God, Shane!" I shout as my orgasm crashes over me in wave after delicious wave. I rake my fingers through his hair as he keeps on sucking. My whole body trembles and instinctively, I pull at his hair, trying to pull his head away, but he has his powerful forearms clamped around my thighs still and his head buried in my pussy and I am powerless to move him even an inch. I close my eyes and push my head against the pillow because I realize what he's trying to do. When the sensitivity passes and I stop struggling, he releases one of my legs and runs his warm hand from my knee up my inner thigh before pushing two fingers deep inside me, and I swear I almost pass out. I groan so loudly and so wantonly that it makes him growl loudly. Curling his fingers deep inside, he pushes against my G-spot and I feel the intense pressure building in my abdomen.

"Shane!" I breathe as my orgasm rushes out of me in an intense rush of fluid that makes him groan in appreciation.

"I love how hard you come for me, Hacker."

I manage to look down as my head spins and I pant for breath. "You've soaked the bedsheets."

"No, *you've* soaked the bedsheets, sweetheart." He wipes his jaw and mouth with one swipe of a large hand as he moves up the bed. "With your sweet cum."

Heat flushes over my chest and neck as he slides his fingers out of me and the wet sound echoes around the room.

"I've thought about this every day since you left, Jessie. About seeing your body. Touching it. Tasting it," he says as he stares down at me as his face glistens with my arousal. His hands slide over my breasts and he squeezes them hard, making me moan again. "It feels even better than I remember."

"Shane!" I pant as he keeps kneading my soft flesh in his hands and tugging my nipples.

"Do you have any idea how cruel it is to have a taste of this body, and then have it taken away, never knowing if you will ever get it again?" he growls as he stares down at me, his eyes roaming over my body like a hungry lion about to feast on his kill.

"Yes," I pant. "Because I had a taste of yours too."

He leans down, resting his weight on his forearms as he nestles between my thighs and nudges his cock at my dripping wet entrance. "Were you a good girl while you were away in Arizona, Hacker?" he arches an eyebrow at me.

Arizona? What the hell? That seems so far away now. "Of course I was," I blink at him.

"Good. Because if I ever find out anyone else has touched you, I will skin him alive."

Fuck! His possessiveness is so hot! "Have you been good too?" I groan.

He cocks his head to the side as though he's thinking about his answer.

"Shane?"

He grins at me and then with a roll of his hips, he thrusts his cock inside me, so hard that I shift a few inches up the bed. "There's been no one but you, Hacker," he growls, taking my wrists and pinning them down as he nails me to the bed. "Because you and this cunt have ruined me."

I suck in a sharp breath as he slams into me. "Damn! You feel so good. I've missed your cock."

He buries his head against my neck and slows his pace. "Just my cock?"

"Hmm, and your mouth. And maybe your fingers too. But that's all," I breathe as I wrap my legs around his waist, drawing him closer and deeper.

He sucks on that sweet spot on my neck that he knows drives me crazy and slams into me again. "You sure?" he growls.

I experience another sudden rush of wet heat and tears prick my eyes as another orgasm threatens to overwhelm me. "You know I've missed everything, Shane. I love you so much."

"Fuck, Jessie," he hisses as he drives harder and I wonder if he heard what I just said. "I can't get far enough inside of you, sweetheart. Your pussy was made for me."

I rake my nails down his back as my entire body screams for release. "Please, Shane," I beg him even though I don't know what I'm begging for. I have never been fucked harder in my life. Our breathing comes hard and fast. Sweat slicks our bodies as we grasp at each other, desperate to sate the insatiable craving. Stars flicker behind my eyelids as he brings me close to the edge of complete oblivion. And just when I am about to tip over, he lifts his head from my neck, pinning my hands beside my head and lacing his fingers through mine. He presses his forehead against mine as he slows his pace, making me groan loudly in frustration.

"Not yet, Jessie," he growls.

"You are a devil," I pant as I gasp for breath. I squeeze my legs tighter around his waist as my walls squeeze his cock, but he continues his delicious torment, fucking me so slowly but somehow reaching even deeper than before, until every cell in my body trembles with the need for some release.

"You have fucking destroyed me, Hacker," he groans and his hips drive deeper inside me, hitting that perfect sweet spot at the exact angle with the perfect amount of pressure and my climax tears through my body like black powder. He seals his mouth over mine, swallowing every moan and whimper as I ride the waves of euphoria. When I feel like I might pass out from lack of oxygen, he throws his head back and shouts my name as he finds his own release and then he kisses me again as we take everything from each other, kissing and grinding our bodies until there is nothing left to give.

He pulls back, and we stare at each other, panting for breath. "I think I just blacked out," I breathe.

"You *only* blacked out? I think my soul just left my body," he pants, making me laugh.

He pulls out of me and rolls onto his back, pulling me with him so that I am lying on his chest with his arms wrapped around me. He runs his fingers gently up and down my back, and his heartbeat thrums against my ear. I sigh contentedly as I snuggle closer to him.

"Did you mean what you said before, Jessie?" he asks softly.

I tilt my head to look at him. "That I love you?" I whisper. I wasn't sure if he'd heard me over the sound of his growling.

"Yes."

I shift my body slightly, so I can look directly into his eyes. "Of course I meant it. I never stopped, Shane."

His eyes narrow as they search my face. He opens his mouth to speak but then he closes it again.

"It's okay," I say as I brush his hair from his face. "You don't have to say it back." I am so desperate to hear the words, but even if he is not ready to say them, I feel it anyway.

"Those three words," he breathes, and my racing heart stops beating.

Please don't fuck this up after what we just did, Shane!

He brushes his fingertips over my cheeks. "They don't feel like enough. For this. For you."

"But they are."

"Then I love you, Jessie Ryan," he whispers.

TWENTY-FOUR

As I reach for the jar of peanut butter on the top shelf, the pain shoots through my neck and shoulders. "Fuck," I hiss as I pull my hand back and rub the back of my neck. "Why the fuck do we put this shit up so high?" I snap.

"Erm. Because we're all like six foot two. Except Jessie, obviously, and I like to watch her stretching for things," Mikey chuckles as he sits at the kitchen island behind me. "And I told you I would make your sandwich, bro."

"I can make it myself," I snap at him, frustrated by the pain and the limits it places on my body. I wince as I roll my shoulder. I probably shouldn't have pushed myself so much in the gym earlier, but as soon as the doctor approved me for some light cardio, I couldn't wait to get back in there. Like I had some point to prove, if only to myself. I shake my head in annoyance. I only did a one-mile walk at the pace of a fucking limp tortoise.

"Suit yourself," Mikey snaps.

"Are you boys fighting again?" Shane says from behind us and I spin around as fast as my body allows to see my oldest brother walking into the kitchen with the biggest smile I have ever seen on his face. We all figured he was home when we saw his bags in the hallway, and when we couldn't find Jessie, well it wasn't hard to figure out where the two of them were. I for one, am relieved that they have sorted their shit out, and from the expression on his face, they have been doing it all afternoon.

"Shane!" I say with a grin as Mikey jumps up from his stool and wraps him in a giant bear hug.

"Okay. I was only gone a week," Shane laughs but he hugs Mikey back just as fiercely. We have all been through so much these past few months, it has seemed like a lifetime. Now that we are all back under the same roof, and things are good with him and Jessie, maybe things can start getting back to some sort of normal around here.

When Mikey finally lets Shane go, our oldest brother walks over to me. "You're looking great, kid," he says with a twinkle in his eye.

"Feeling great," I nod.

"You weren't saying that when you couldn't reach the peanut butter ten seconds ago," Mikey laughs.

"Asshole!"

Shane laughs and then he wraps his arms around me too, making sure not to squeeze me too hard. "It's good to have you back, bro," I say in his ear.

"It's good to be back," he replies as he takes a step back. "You making PB and jelly sandwiches?"

"No. Mikey is," I wink at my twin who rolls his eyes and walks over to us.

"Out of my way then," he says, and I shuffle over to the kitchen island.

"So, where is Jessie, Shane?" Mikey asks as Shane takes a stool beside me.

"Power napping," he replies.

Mikey spins around and grins widely at him. "Fuck! You wore her out already?"

"Don't be crass, Michael." He flashes an eyebrow before smiling. "But yeah, I kinda did. So you'd better make her a sandwich too, and I'll take it in to her. You know how cranky she gets when she's hungry."

Mikey laughs out loud before he turns back around to continue making sandwiches.

"You two good now, then?" I ask.

Shane turns to me and nods. "Yeah. We're good, kid."

"Good." I smile at him because him and Jessie being good means we're all good.

"You don't mind if I steal her for the night, do you?" he says this louder so Mikey can hear him too.

"No. Not at all," I reply.

"Your need is greater than mine, bro," Mikey adds.

"Good. Where is Conor?" Shane asks.

"He's downstairs meeting with some new suppliers. But he saw you were back and assumed you were going to be otherwise engaged for most of the afternoon. He said he'll catch up with you later."

"Oh," he frowns.

"I'm pretty sure he won't mind you stealing Jessie away, either. We're all glad you two are sorting your shit out."

"You've all been talking about us then?" Shane arches an eyebrow at me.

Mikey walks over to us, carrying a plate with a sandwich on it. He hands it to me with a grin before he answers Shane's question. "Yep. When we saw your bags in the hall and couldn't find either of you, we figured you were fucking each other senseless."

Shane gives me a feather light slap on the back of my head.

"Oi! I never said anything."

"Yeah, but I can't reach him and don't you two feel each other's pain or something?" he grins.

"Are you forgetting I almost died a week ago," I say, rubbing the spot dramatically.

Mikey rolls his eyes. "How much longer are you going to dine out on this almost dying thing? It's a good thing you're back, Shane, because Liam has been doing some major slacking off. Lying around all day, eating Cheetos and watching Netflix."

Shane shakes his head in mock disgust. "Disgraceful," he says as he takes one half of my sandwich from my plate and takes a huge bite.

"Actually," I say with a dramatic sigh. "I'm feeling kind of dizzy after that nasty blow to the head. I think I might need Jessie to look after me tonight, after all."

Shane turns and narrows his eyes at me while Mikey howls laughing in the background. "You wouldn't?"

"You've just assaulted me and stole my fucking sandwich. Watch me, bro. All I'd have to do is tell her I'm not feeling too good and she'll be in my bed all night long." I wink at him.

"If you weren't still recovering from your near death experience, I would kick your ass right now." Shane scowls before he shoves the rest of my sandwich into his mouth.

"Jessie!" I croak, and Shane glares at me.

"What?" she says as she strolls into the kitchen, taking us all by surprise. She walks straight over to me and drapes an arm around my shoulders, and I can't help but grin at Shane. Before she walked in here, looking good enough to eat in just one of his t-shirts and probably fuck all else, me talking about making her spend the night with me was just a joke, but now he's not sure if all bets are off. Because every single man in this kitchen would fuck her where she stands given half the chance.

She traces a fingertip over the fading bruise on my cheek. "Are you okay?"

I wrap an arm around her waist and pull her close to me and I can sense the frustration coming from my older brother in waves now. "I'm fine, baby. I was just playing with Shane," I say as I brush her hair back from her face before I look past her and wink at him.

"Don't upset him. You know how he gets," she whispers, but clearly loud enough for him to hear.

Shane stands up and pushes his stool back. Standing behind her, he wraps her hair around his fist and tilts her head slightly. "I'm going to make you pay for that later, sweetheart," he growls in her ear and she shivers against me making my cock twitch in my shorts.

As Shane moves closer to her, he presses her body further into mine. "Jessie," I groan as my cock stiffens. "If you don't stop pressing up against me like that, I'm going to have to make you do something about this situation you're causing here." I glance down at my groin.

She opens her mouth in surprise, but she knows exactly what she does to all of us with her hot little body. "I only just walked in here. I am not responsible for that," she says as she looks down too.

Shane peers over her shoulder, glancing down at the outline of my hard cock in my shorts, still with his hand fisted in her hair. "Well, I'm certainly not responsible for it, sweetheart," he laughs softly before he releases her hair and checks his watch. "I'm going downstairs to check in with Conor." Then he places his hand under Jessie's chin, turning her face slightly until she's looking directly at him. "I'll be back up here in one hour. I want you in my bed. Naked," he orders and then he glances back at my cock and rolls his eyes. "And showered," he adds before he kisses her softly.

Shane takes the other half of my sandwich and winks at me. "Thanks for the food, boys," he says before he walks out of the room, leaving Jessie alone with us — for one whole hour.

I pull her between my thighs and wrap my other arm around her too. "So?" I arch one eyebrow at her.

"So, what?" She bites her lip, and I want to bite it too.

"You know what, baby."

"You're supposed to be taking it easy, Liam," she breathes. "You already did too much in the gym this morning."

"I will take it easy, baby. I'll fuck you real slow," I say as I drop my head and trail kisses along her collarbone and onto her neck because it drives her crazy.

"Liam," she pants, and it has been way too long since I heard her say my name like that. I stand up and lift her onto the counter, ignoring the searing pain that shoots through my arms and torso when I do. She places her hands on my shoulders and looks at me with those beautiful blue eyes as I slip my hands beneath her t-shirt until I reach her panties. "I'm surprised you're wearing these," I say softly as I pull them down over her hips.

She wiggles her ass to help me get them off easier and shakes her head. "I always wear panties around the house."

"Oh, so it's just when you're lying in bed watching movies with me that you don't, then? Don't think I haven't noticed you teasing me this past week, baby."

"That was one time because I'd just got out of the shower," she says as her cheeks flush pink. "I have not been teasing you."

"Hmm?" I shake my head. "What do you think, Mikey? Is Jessie a tease?"

Mikey walks around the kitchen island to where we are with his plate and sandwich in his hand, and takes a seat. "You're both teasing me right now," he says with a flash of his eyebrows. "Because you know I've gotta get to work soon. So, hurry up and fuck her, bro, so I can at least watch the whole show."

Jessie's cheeks turn an even deeper shade of pink, which only makes me laugh because me and my twin have fucked her together, and watched her being fucked more times than I can count, but I love that it still makes her blush.

"And take off her top. Amateur," he shakes his head and takes a bite of his sandwich.

I wink at Jessie as I reach for her t-shirt and she lifts her arms obligingly, allowing me to pull it off and over her head before I throw it at my annoying brother. Once she's naked, I wrap my arms around her waist and pull her toward me. "How long has it been since I fucked you?" I whisper in her ear.

"I don't know. A little over a week?" she offers.

"Almost two weeks, Jessie. So this is way overdue," I groan as I line my cock up at her wet entrance and she moans softly. Her body is flush against mine and her nipples are hard against my chest as I run my hands over her beautiful soft skin. I am so hard for her; I'm not going to last much longer.

"Liam," she groans as she rocks her hips against me.

"You want fucking, baby?"

"Yes," she gasps as I thrust my hips forward and drive my cock into her tight, wet pussy and my balls immediately draw up into my stomach and I have to grind my teeth together and think of anything but her to hold off from blowing my load in her right now. Her walls squeeze me tight and I moan into her neck before I drop my head lower, sucking one of her pebbled nipples into my mouth as I slide one hand from her back and down to her clit and rub — slowly but with plenty of pressure because that is the quickest way to get her off. If I'm coming fast, then so is she. I keep sucking on her nipples, holding her tight to me as I rail into her. I tried to go slow but I can't help it. I can't get deep enough inside her.

"Oh! Liam!" she groans as she rakes her nails down my back, somehow managing to avoid my stitches because she knows where all of my wounds are. She has taken care of me so well this past week. I don't know what I'd have done without her.

"I've missed this sweet pussy, baby," I mumble against her skin.

"I've missed you too. You feel so good," she pants as her walls tighten around me and I feel her on the edge and thank the heavens because I am about to come and I can't stop myself. I empty myself inside her while she teeters on the precipice of her own release. I suck and rub and fuck her harder until she moans my name loudly, her legs trembling as she comes for me.

I press my forehead against hers. "That was incredible, baby," I pant, even though every single part of my body is aching and sore. But it was so fucking worth it.

"It was," she smiles at me and I kiss her softly and then have to force myself to pull my dick out of her because as much as I enjoy pushing Shane's buttons, I wouldn't deprive him of a night with our girl after everything he's been doing for us these past few weeks.

"That was quite the show," Mikey nods his approval as I help Jessie down from the counter. He takes the last bite of his sandwich and holds out her t-shirt to her.

"Thank you," she whispers.

"My pleasure, Red. Now come here."

She pulls on her top while I pull up my shorts and she takes the few steps toward him before he pulls her into his arms and kisses her softly. I watch as he slips his tongue inside her mouth and then he just kisses her with his arms wrapped around her waist. When they finally come up for air, he stares at her. "I love you so fucking much. You know that, right?"

"Yes," she breathes. "I love you too."

His smile takes over his whole face and I realize I am witnessing my idiot twin completely and utterly in love for the first time in his life. I mean, I already knew he loved her, but fuck, he *really* loves her. The moment is broken when he catches me staring at the two of them and rolls his eyes before slapping her on the ass and making her squeal. "You'd better go take a shower before Shane comes back."

She nods. "Yeah. I will."

"There's a sandwich on the counter for you."

"Thank you."

"And don't forget, you and me have got a date in the gym tomorrow morning. I'm gonna have you bench pressing your personal best before the week is out."

"I won't forget," she smiles at him.

CHAPTER

TWENTY-FIVE

JESSIE

After I've showered and slathered myself in cocoa and vanilla body butter, I lie in Shane's bed waiting for him. The cotton sheets are soft and cool against my hot skin and I stretch like a cat, feeling so content that I could purr like one right now too. Shane is a complicated, moody asshole, but he is my asshole, and it seems like we are finally back on track. I glance at the clock and notice it's been over an hour since he left the kitchen to see Conor. Is this some sort of test from him? Is he trying to see how long I'm going to lie here waiting for him? I turn on my side and reach for my phone, just as he walks through the door.

"Hey," I smile at him.

His eyes are dark as he glares at me and I wonder what I've done to make him mad now when I haven't even seen him since the kitchen.

"Are you naked under there, Hacker?" he growls, and I realize he's not mad at all. Just horny.

"Of course," I whisper. "And freshly showered. Just like you told me."

He arches one eyebrow at me. "It's not like you to do as you're told so easily, though."

"Were you hoping I'd disobey you?" I purr as the wet heat sears between my thighs.

"No," he shakes his head as he peels his t-shirt over his head. "I don't need a reason to spank your ass, Jessie."

"Good," I whisper as he stalks toward the bed. "Was Conor okay?"

"Yes. Just busy. I didn't get much chance to chat with him. I'll catch up with him tomorrow."

"Oh?" I bite my lip. So where the hell has he been?

"What?" he frowns at me.

"You were gone for a while, is all. Longer than an hour."

He crawls onto the bed, holding himself over me. "Erin called. I had to discuss some urgent business with her."

Her name is a like a dagger to my heart. I know that I shouldn't let her get to me, but she is always there in the background. Making me feel like I don't belong with him.

"Jessie!" He shoots me a look that makes goosebumps prickle along my forearms.

"What?" I frown. "She was with you on your trip too, wasn't she? I thought you two would have sorted all of your business out then."

He closes his eyes and I see him take a deep breath, as though he's trying to get his temper under control. "She came to Chicago with me. For one night. That was it."

"Did she share your hotel room?" I ask, even though I get that I'm being petty and childish, because he wouldn't be here with me now if he was screwing Erin.

"Don't!" he says with a sigh.

"That's not an answer, Shane."

"That's because it's a stupid fucking question, Jessie."

Damn! He was right earlier. We do screw everything up when we talk.

"It's not stupid to me," I whisper, and his face softens slightly.

"Of course she didn't share my room. Erin is a good lawyer, Jessie. She has worked for me and my family for years. She's going to be in my life, but there will never be anything between us like that. I need you to find a way to be okay with that, because I can't keep having these conversations with you."

"I am okay with it. I will be. It's just that she's so damn beautiful and elegant — like this graceful swan, while I'm a..." I trail off, unsure of what I am compared to her.

"You're a what?" he arches one eyebrow at me.

"A penguin!" I offer.

Shane presses his lips together as he tries to stop himself from laughing, but it has certainly diffused the tension between us. "What kind of penguin?" he eventually asks with a frown.

"I don't know. One of those little dumpy ones you see in the zoo."

"I happen to think they're adorable," he laughs openly now.

"It's not funny, Shane," I make a feeble protest. "I'm trying to explain how she makes me feel."

He sucks the air through his teeth as he stares down at me. "I have touched, kissed and tasted every part of your body, Jessie. I can hardly keep my hands off you. You've got my cock weeping to get inside you here, sweetheart. Whether you think of yourself as a swan, a penguin or a fucking pigeon, do you honestly believe that I don't worship every single inch of you? I want you so fucking much." He growls out the last words, and I feel them deep in my core.

"I know," I whisper as his rock hard cock twitches against my abdomen through the thin sheet as though to confirm what he's just said.

"So, can we make sure Erin never comes between us again?"

"I just don't understand how you can feel nothing for her," I admit.

"Why?" he frowns.

"Because you were in love with her once?"

"Yes. So?"

"I've never been in love before now, but I don't understand how once you've loved someone, you won't always love them on some level. I can't imagine ever not loving you. Even when I was desperate to hate you, I couldn't."

He brushes my hair from my face. "I guess some people's stories are only written in the sand. And some are written in the stars."

Before I can ask where our story is written, he seals his mouth over mine and slides his tongue between my lips. Our mouths mesh together as he swirls his tongue against mine, and the wet heat rushes between my thighs. My hands fist in his hair as he holds my face still while he claims my mouth. I remember how long it took him to first kiss me on the lips and how much I have missed the taste of him. Running my hands down his muscular back and beneath the band of his sweatpants, I slide them over his perfectly toned ass. I groan in frustration as he reaches back and moves them, pinning them either side of my head instead. I spread my legs further apart, so he slips between my thighs and I groan into his mouth as his rock hard cock presses against my pussy. I grind myself on him, desperate to feel him inside me, but he just keeps kissing me until I'm aching for him.

I wrench my lips away from his. "Shane! Why are you punishing me?" I groan.

He pulls his head back and stares down at me. "Kissing me is a punishment?"

"Not at all! But denying me the rest of you is."

He smiles before brushing his nose along my throat and my jawline. "Maybe I'm punishing myself, Hacker?"

"If you are, then please don't. I want all of you, Shane."

"Even the dark parts?" he asks softly.

"Especially those. I want every bit of you. The light and the shade."

I hear the groan rumbling through his chest and throat before he pushes himself up onto his knees and pulls his sweatpants down until his beautiful cock springs free. Then he pulls the covers off of me, making me shiver with excitement and anticipation. I help him by wriggling my legs out and wrapping them around his waist.

'I could fuck you like this forever, sweetheart,' he whispers as he drives his cock into me and I moan loudly, hoping that he'll do just that.

TWENTY-SIX

SHANE

She is gone when I wake up. I slept much later than usual, but it still hurt like hell when I realize she isn't there. Pulling on my sweatpants, I walk down the hallway to the kitchen. My pulse quickens when I see her standing there, leaning against the kitchen island in her yoga pants and sports bra, sipping a cup of coffee.

She looks up and smiles at me and my cock twitches to attention.

"Good morning," she says sweetly.

"Morning, Hacker." I walk over to her and take the coffee mug from her hands, taking a gulp before I place it on the counter behind her. "Why didn't you wake me?" I arch an eyebrow at her.

"You looked so peaceful. Snoring and drooling onto your pillow." She flashes me a wicked grin. "I didn't want to disturb you."

Fuck! I have missed her smart mouth. "I do not snore. Or drool," I growl as I slide my hands around her waist.

She tilts her head. "Well, I guess you'll never know. But you did look peaceful. And I promised Mikey I'd meet him in the gym this morning before he had to go upstate today. He wanted to put me through my paces. Hence, me being all sweaty and disgusting."

"Mikey put you through your paces, huh?" I drop my head to her neck and trail kisses along her throat, making her groan softly. Her skin is salty and sweet and I want to lick every inch of her.

"Not those sort of paces, you deviant," she giggles.

Lifting my head up, I stare into her bright blue eyes, and they sparkle with mischief. She is a world away from the woman who was last in this house two months earlier and I couldn't be happier about that fact. Maybe her time alone in Arizona was exactly what she needed? "I'm a deviant?" I narrow my eyes at her.

"Yes," she purrs.

"Hmm," I slide my hands into the waistband of her yoga pants and my cock throbs in appreciation as I find she's not wearing panties. Her pants glide easily over her ass and down over her thighs as I work my hands inside them.

"Shane, what are you doing?" She stares into my eyes.

"Taking off your pants."

"Why?" she breathes as I slide them further down her legs.

"So I can fuck you."

"What? Here in the kitchen?"

"Well, since you left me without waking me this morning without even a kiss, what choice do I have but to take you wherever I can get you?" I growl as I lift her up onto the counter and continue peeling her pants down her legs until they are completely off. My hands travel up to her sports bra and she lifts her arms in compliance as I pull it off over her head and toss it onto the floor.

"For the record, I did kiss you. But you were out of it. And, we cannot have sex on the counter where everyone is about to come eat their breakfast."

"Why not?" I grin as I wrap my arms around her naked body and kiss her neck.

I love the way she tilts her head back to give me easier access whenever I kiss a certain spot. "Because we'll be in their way, and it's unhygienic," she says in a feeble protest as her hands run over my back and she pulls me closer. She is so soft and warm and I contemplate carrying her back to bed and staying there for the rest of the day — but I have work to do now that I'm back.

"But, you are my breakfast, Hacker. And everyone in this house has eaten your cunt and your ass, and they will have absolutely no problem with you dripping your cum on here."

"Shane," she hisses as her neck flushes with heat, making me chuckle.

"Jessie," I reply as I pull my sweatpants down enough to allow my cock to spring free. I run one of my hands down to her cunt and stifle a groan as I feel her slick heat. I could bury myself in her forever and it still wouldn't be enough. "I went without being inside you for almost three months, sweetheart. You don't get to leave me in bed all alone unless I say you can. And later, I'm going to spank that beautiful ass of yours for doing it today."

She groans as I push two fingers inside her and her walls clench around me. Fuck! I almost forgot how much my girl loves a spanking.

"Shane!" she groans again and the sound of my name on her lips sends all the blood rushing straight to my groin. I pull my fingers out of her and drive my cock into her instead.

She wraps her legs around my waist and clings to me as I fuck her. I'm so lost in her, I don't notice Conor walk into the room. But she does and her body tenses.

"I see you two have made up?" he says as he sits a few feet away from us at the kitchen island and pours a bowl of muesli before topping it with some milk from the counter.

"Yeah," I grunt.

"Shane!" Jessie hisses in my ear.

"What? Conor has seen me fucking you before."

"I know," she breathes, but she looks at him. He's sitting there with his head bent low, scrolling through his phone. "He looks pissed," she whispers.

"He's not pissed. He's tired," I growl as I press her closer to me and bite down on her neck until she moans, but she's still distracted by him. I'd ask him to join us, but he looks exhausted and he's hardly stopped working since he got back from Arizona almost two weeks ago.

I press my lips against her ear. "If you don't stop looking at him instead of me, I will spread you open on this counter and eat your cunt while he eats his fucking cereal."

Conor laughs softly as he keeps his head bent low, and she turns back to me. "Sorry," she breathes.

"I'm going to leave you two alone and take my breakfast to go," Conor says as he stands up and walks out of the room. Once he's gone, she relaxes into my arms again and I fuck her until she shouts my name. When I find my own release, I stand there with her, my dick still inside her and my arms wrapped around her waist as she breathes against my neck.

"What was that about, Hacker?"

"What?" She looks up at me and stares at me with her bright blue eyes.

"You were acting weird when Conor came in."

"Oh," she blushes. "It's just I've hardly seen him since we got back from Arizona. Between him working so much and me looking after Liam, I haven't spent much time with him."

"We've all been busy and distracted."

"I know. It just seemed like he was pissed then, that's all." She bites her lip. "We were so close on the drive back to New York, and now it seems like there's a little distance between us."

"He was just tired. He's been working non-stop since he got back."

She nods and chews on her lip and looks so damn beautiful it makes me want to take her to my bed and never let her leave. "Jessie?" I breathe. I can't believe I'm going to ask her this question, but I have to know the answer.

"Yeah?"

"Would you have come back from Arizona if it was me who came for you instead of Conor?"

She doesn't hesitate for even a second. "Yes."

The rush of love I feel for her almost knocks me off my feet. I narrow my eyes at her. "You sure?"

She places her hands on my face. "One hundred percent. I mean, I would have made you work a little harder for it," she grins at me. "But I would go anywhere with you, Shane Ryan. You think I don't have a connection with you like I do Conor and the twins, but you're wrong. You're a hard person to get close to, but you push me in ways no one else can."

"Just don't let me push you too far, Hacker, because I hated every second you were away from us."

"I won't," she smiles. "You are never getting rid of me again. I swear on my life."

I swallow hard as I think about the apology I owe her. "I need to talk to you about what happened the last time you were here. In the basement."

"When you hate-fucked me?" She arches an eyebrow at me.

I wrap my arms tighter around her. "I'd call it angry fucking, but yeah. And also for those things I said."

"When you called me a whore?" She bites her lip seduc-

151

tively while I'm filled with shame and remorse. I had no right to call her that, no matter what I thought she'd done.

"Yes," I nod. "You know I was just angry, and I don't really think that, right?"

"Hmm." She presses her lips together and tilts her head to one side as though she's considering whether to accept my apology, even though I know she forgave me for it a long time ago. But it still needed to be said.

"And for what happened after that too. I'm so fucking sorry, sweetheart."

She presses a soft kiss against my throat. "Well, I accept your apology for calling me a whore, and for leaving me alone in that horrible cell, because that was an asshole move. But the angry fucking was super hot."

"Hmm. It definitely was," I chuckle against her skin.

"In fact, it was so hot, that I intend to purposely make you pissed at me on a regular basis."

"That could be a very dangerous move, Hacker." I scrape my teeth along her jawline.

"I hope so," she purrs. We stand in silence for a few seconds before she speaks again. "I'm sorry too, Shane. I know how much it took for you to let me in. I know I let you down. But I never lied. Everything I felt. Everything I told you was real."

"I know, Jessie," I say, kissing her on the forehead. "You want to go clean up and check on him?"

"Would you mind?"

I pull my cock out of her and a rush of our cum dribbles onto the counter. Fuck! This girl is going to end me. "No. I've got some work to do anyway. I'm going to clean up your mess," I look down between her thighs. "Then I'll grab some breakfast and a shower. I'll be in my office all day so come find me when you're done."

"I think you'll find you are the one responsible for the

mess." She flashes an eyebrow as I help her down from the counter and she picks up her clothes. "But thank you for taking care of it." She pushes up onto her tiptoes and wraps her arms around my neck before she presses her lips softly against mine. "I love you," she murmurs against me and I can't help but smile.

I smack her on the ass. "You too. Now go see Conor before he goes to sleep."

She walks out of the kitchen, swaying her hips and that perfect peach of an ass as she clutches her clothes in her hands. "Put your clothes on after you clean up, Hacker. He needs some sleep!" I shout after her.

"Will do, Sir," she shouts back and my cock twitches to life.

Sir? Fuck me! I could get used to that.

TWENTY-SEVEN

I take a super quick shower and throw some underwear and one of Shane's t-shirts on before I walk along the hallway to Conor's bedroom. I don't knock in case he's already fallen asleep and I don't want to wake him if he has. Pushing open the door, I step inside to find him lying in bed, but he's still awake.

"Jessie?" He blinks at me as I walk closer to him.

"Hey." I chew on my lip. Not even sure what I want to say.

"I'm really fucking tired, Angel. Can this wait until later?"

I swallow hard and maybe it's the expression on my face, but he holds out his hand. "Come here," he says, and I walk over to the bed and sit beside him.

"I know you're tired. I just haven't seen you for a few days and I wanted to make sure we were okay?"

He reaches up and brushes my hair back from my face. "Of course we are. Why wouldn't we be?"

"I don't know. We shared a lot of stuff while we were on the road. I've never felt that close to anyone before. But since we got back..." I shrug. "I kind of feel like there's some distance between us. But am I just imagining it?"

He frowns at me, his beautiful brown eyes as dark as coal. "Take off the clothes, Angel, and get in here."

"What? No. You're tired. I just-"

"Take it all off, Jessie. Now!" he commands.

I do as he tells me, peeling off the clothes that I've only just put on, and I climb into bed beside him. He holds out an arm and I lie on his chest before he wraps his huge biceps around me. "Do you think I'm pissed because I walked in on you and Shane fucking?"

"It kind of seemed like you were."

"I love watching you being fucked by my brothers. But I'm fucking exhausted, Angel. I've been working sixteen hour days to catch up in the club. I also got you all to myself for five days, and I know how much Shane and the twins have missed you. I'm sorry if I've neglected you, but there is no distance between us, Angel. None at all." He plants a kiss on the top of my head. "But I do need some fucking sleep. So now that you're here, you're going to have to lie here with me until I doze off, because I fucking love falling asleep with your hot, naked body on me," he groans as he closes his eyes.

I smile as I press my cheek against his chest and listen to the soothing rhythm of his soft breathing as he drifts off to sleep.

CHAPTER

TWENTY-EIGHT

JESSIE

As soon as Conor is sleeping soundly, I untangle myself from his warm body and slide out of bed. Grabbing my underwear and Shane's t-shirt from the floor, I get dressed quietly, careful not to disturb him. I turn and look at him before I slip out of the door. He looks so peaceful and content, and I'm overwhelmed by a rush of pure love for him.

I close his door softly behind me and make my way down the hall to Shane's office and find him as I always used to in here. Head bent low over his computer and a slight frown on his handsome face.

"Has anyone ever told you, you work too hard?" I say as I walk into the room and sit opposite him.

He looks up with a devilish grin on his face that makes my insides melt like chocolate. "How else am I supposed to distract myself, Hacker? If I didn't have my work to keep me busy, you would never leave my bed."

I smile at the thought of being a permanent resident of his bed. Shane Ryan and his brothers make me constantly horny. I shake my head. I am not here for that. Not right now, anyway. "I thought that maybe now Liam's no longer on bed rest, I could..." I chew on my lip because Shane Ryan makes me nervous as hell, but for all the right reasons.

He closes his laptop and leans forward in his seat, narrowing his eyes at me. "Thought you could what?" he asks in that low gravelly voice that vibrates through my bones.

"Maybe I could pull my weight a little more around here. Help you out with those contracts you're working on. Or anything really? I'd like to get more involved in the business, if that's okay?" I whisper.

He sucks in a breath and sits back in his chair. "You want to be more involved in the family business?" He arches an eyebrow at me.

"Yes."

"Why?" He frowns and suddenly I get the sense that this is some sort of test.

"Well, it kind of makes sense, seeing as we're..." I swallow hard.

He reaches across his desk and takes hold of my hand, brushing his fingertips across my palm and sending skitters of electricity shooting up my forearm. "We're your family too?" he finishes my sentence for me.

I lift my gaze to meet his, for a second worrying that I have made an assumption that I shouldn't have and overstepped. But his eyes are burning into mine, full of emotion and longing, and I realize he needs assurance about what we are, just as much as I do. "Yes," I whisper.

I'm rewarded with one of his genuine, killer smiles before he lifts my fingers to his lips and kisses the tips softly. It's such a tender act from him that I am completely blindsided. I rarely see this side of him, and I realize how privileged I am to be allowed to, when he is vulnerable and laid bare for me. The electricity in the room is palpable now. My breath catches in my throat as he continues pressing soft kisses against my fingers that send jolts of warmth and pleasure coursing through my body. The familiar wet heat is beginning to build in my core and I shift in my seat, squeezing my thighs together to quell the growing need. He reads me so well, as though he has known me forever. Gently placing my hand back on his desk, he leans back in his chair. "We'd better get to work, Hacker. Because if you keep looking at me like that, we won't get anything done."

"Why not?" I purr as I lean forward, closing the distance between us again, even though I know exactly what he means because whenever we are in a room together, the air is supercharged with sexual electricity.

He leans back in too, until he is so close that I can smell his incredible scent — cologne, sex and masculinity. "Because I will have you naked and bent over my desk in about ten seconds flat. So, stop with the flirting. Pull your chair around and fire up the desktop. We've got lots of business to catch up on."

The wicked twinkle in his eyes makes me laugh softly. "You're so bossy," I say, pushing myself up from the chair and wheeling it around to his side of the desk. I place it next to his, so it's close but not touching and sit back down. Flexing my fingers and my shoulders, I switch on the desktop just as Shane grabs hold of my chair and pulls it toward his, until they are flush together. I smile at the screen as I resist the urge to turn and look at him, but I can see him watching me from the corner of my eye.

"Don't be distracting me now. I have lots of work to do," I say as I continue staring at the screen.

He laughs softly. "I'm distracting you, Hacker? You're the one walking around here in just your underwear and my shirt. How the fuck am I supposed to concentrate?"

"Would you like me to go get changed?" I breathe, still refusing to look him in the eye.

"Fuck, no," he growls. "Now get to work."

TWENTY-NINE

JESSIE

I'm still sitting in Shane's office when Conor saunters into the room with a huge smile on his face. He's been in bed for over ten hours. He's wearing just a pair of shorts and his magnificent torso is on full display as he stretches and yawns. "That was a fucking epic sleep," he groans.

"Glad to see you're back in the land of the living," Shane smiles at him.

Conor nods. "The twins are helping me out tonight, so you two will have the place to yourselves." He walks to the sofa and flops down onto it.

"Liam too?" I ask.

"Yes." Conor rolls his eyes. "He's desperate to feel useful, so I promised him he could do some paperwork in the office for me. I'll keep an eye on him the whole time. Don't worry."

"Now that he's back on his feet, there will be no stopping him, Jessie," Shane says with a smile. "You might need to distract him a little more to keep him up here in the apartment."

"Fuck! I wish the Russians had kidnapped me this time," Conor says and both he and Shane laugh out loud.

"That's not funny!" I reprimand them and try to stop myself from smiling, because it is so good to see them laughing together like this.

"Come here, Angel," Conor says, and I walk over to him before he pulls me down onto the sofa, so I'm sitting with my legs over his lap. "We're just kidding. We promise never to let anyone kidnap us. Okay?"

I roll my eyes and shake my head as they continue laughing.

Shane's cell phone rings and he answers it, leaving Conor and I to talk between ourselves. "I'm sorry if I seemed distant this morning," he says, brushing the hair back from my face.

"You weren't. I know you're busy. I just miss you."

"I miss you too. I have to work again tonight, but then I'll take tomorrow off, and you and I can spend the day and night together. How does that sound?"

"That sounds good." I smile just as Shane ends his phone call and stands up from his chair. He walks toward us and I see him and Conor share a look that I don't quite understand, but that makes goosebumps prickle all over my body.

Suddenly, Conor turns me in his arms, so I am sitting over his lap, facing forward, with my thighs draped over his and my ass against his groin. "We need to talk about this morning, Angel," he murmurs in my ear as Shane reaches us.

"What about this morning?" I say as my pulse thrums against the skin on my throat where his lips are resting.

"I can't have you thinking I'm pissed at you because you're fucking one of my brothers, can I?" he growls as his hands drop to my hips and he spreads his legs wider so that my thighs are now wide open and my ass drops into the open space.

"No," I whisper as my stomach contracts in anticipation. It seems like the two of them are playing a game and I'm not sure of the rules. I know they haven't spoken to each other since this morning because Conor has been asleep all day, and I've been working with Shane, but it seems like they both understand exactly what the other one is thinking.

"Whose is this t-shirt, Angel?" Conor asks as his fingers grip the edge of it.

"Shane's," I breathe as I look up at him standing in front of the two of us.

"Shall we give it back to him?" Conor chuckles as he peels it off while Shane winks at him.

I lift my arms and allow Conor to pull the shirt off over my head before he tosses it onto the floor. Shane remains silent, but he looks down at me the whole time, his dark green eyes blazing with fire.

"I think we need to remind you how this thing between us works, Angel," Conor says as he plants soft kisses against my neck while removing my bra.

"What? Why?" I mumble as my breasts fall free and they can both see how hard my nipples are. Shane's eyes drop to them and he palms his cock through his suit pants. We have been working so hard that we have managed to spend the whole day and early evening together, and for the most part, barely touched. We had an epic make-out session on this sofa after lunch, but we were interrupted by Shane's cell phone ringing. And apart from our hands accidentally brushing, or his knee grazing mine occasionally, we haven't touched each other since. Now, I'm hyper aware of the sexual energy vibrating through the room and the heat pools in my core.

"I suspect our time on the road showed you a little more of my possessive side, Angel. And know that I meant it when I said I would burn down the world for you. I would cut off the hands of any man who touches you, or any body part that he touches you with," Conor says in my ear. "You belong to me. This," he slides his hand beneath my panties and grabs hold of my pussy, "belongs to me."

"Conor," I pant as my eyes are drawn back to Shane, who is glaring at me so hard my skin burns.

"But you belong to my brothers too, Jessie. And I will never be pissed at them for touching you, or at you for wanting them to. It makes me so fucking hard to see you coming for them."

My heart flutters in my chest at Conor's words and I watch in anticipation as Shane's hands move to his belt and he unbuckles it slowly. The sound of him doing that is all that can be heard in the quiet of his office, and the rush of wet heat surges between my thighs. I don't understand what the hell these two are up to, but I already have an idea it is going to be hot and I can hardly wait.

As though he's reading my thoughts as well as Shane's, Conor tells me what is about to happen. "I'm going to hold you down while Shane fucks you, Angel," he growls as he wraps one of his giant arms around me, pulling me back until I'm lying against his chest and my hips are tilted upwards. "And when he makes you come, I'm going to feel every single tremor and whimper just as much as he does."

"Oh, God," I groan as Shane pulls his cock free and drops to his knees in front of me, hooking his thumbs into the side of my panties and pulling them down over my legs until I am bare and open for him.

Conor spreads his legs further apart so that my thighs open even wider and Shane stares at my pussy. "Fucking beautiful, Hacker," he hisses.

Conor slides his free hand over my stomach and down between my legs, stroking my slick folds and dipping one of his fingers inside me, causing me to whimper. "She is so fucking ready for you, Shane," he laughs softly before sliding his finger out and moving his hand up to my neck, where he wraps it around my throat, tilting my head back slightly and holding me tight.

Shane looks behind me and grins at his younger brother while I feel like I might pass out from how turned on I am. I swear I'm going to burst into flames if this gets any hotter. "She's always ready, aren't you, sweetheart?" he winks at me as he places his warm hands on my hips and lines his cock up at my wet entrance.

"Shane," I pant as I wait for him to give me what my body is craving.

He rubs the pad of his thumb over my clit and I try to raise my hips, but he holds me down with his other hand, pressing down on my abdomen while Conor tightens his grip on me, until both of them are holding me firmly in place. "So impatient, Jessie," Shane growls. "Shall we show Conor how I make you squirt?"

The heat flushes over my entire body and I have to close my eyes as the growl rumbles through Conor's chest so fiercely that I experience every tremor. "You've made her squirt too?" he groans as his hard cock twitches against my back.

"Plenty," Shane grins wickedly.

"That's not fair. You're not supposed to talk about this kind of stuff with each other," I whimper in a feeble protest.

"No more talking then," Shane growls. "Shall I just fuck you?"

"Yes," I whimper shamelessly.

"I wish you could see how good you look right now. With Conor holding you wide open for me. Your cunt dripping wet and your thighs trembling while you wait for my cock. Tell me what you want, Jessie. I want to hear you say the words."

My eyes burn into his. I suppose after what happened this morning in the kitchen, this is the perfect way to teach me a lesson. "Fuck me, Shane. Please?" I beg.

He holds onto my hips again as he pushes his cock into me and I moan so loudly I'm sure Mikey and Liam must have heard

163

me at the other end of the apartment. My entire body trembles as he rails into me, while Conor holds me tight. "You think this could ever make me mad, Angel?" he breathes in my ear. "You look fucking incredible being nailed by my brother."

I tilt my head back so I can look at him, but Shane drives harder into me, making me groan his name. "Look at me, Jessie," he commands and I drag my eyes back to him as Conor laughs softly beneath me. "When I'm inside you, I want your eyes on me. Is that clear?" he growls as he continues fucking me so hard that my body presses further and further into Conor's.

"Yes," I breathe.

"Good girl," he says as he bends his head low and sucks one of my hard nipples into his mouth before biting gently and I come with a rush of wet release a few moments before he does. Conor releases his grip on me and as the last of my orgasm rolls through my body, I glance at Shane and experience such a rush of emotion that tears prick at my eyes. Shane Ryan is on his knees before me, completely undone, and Conor is holding onto me like he will never let me go. I can hardly believe that just two weeks ago, I was in Arizona, completely alone and busting my ass in Ray's bar and convincing myself it was what I needed to make me happy. I made myself believe that I didn't need any of this and that I would never feel any of it ever again.

Shane pulls out of me, tucking his cock back into his boxer briefs and zipping up his suit pants before he looks at me again. When he does, I see the concern flash across his face. "You okay?" he asks as he rubs the pad of his thumb over my cheek.

"Better than okay," I nod before drawing in a shaky breath.

"Good," he says with a flash of his eyebrows before leaning in to kiss me softly.

While Shane is kissing me, Conor shifts me slightly on his lap so that he has enough room to take his cock out of his sweatpants before he presses his lips against my ear. "This wasn't part of the plan, and I know you've been fucked non-stop since Shane got back home, but if I don't get inside you now, I think I'll fucking explode. Because you've got me as hard as fucking steel here, Angel. So, slide yourself onto my cock, and I promise I'll take it easy with you."

My pussy is tender and throbbing, but I want him just as much as he wants me. I plant my hands on Shane's shoulders to steady myself, and lift my hips, allowing Conor to guide his cock against my entrance before I sink down onto him.

"Fuck, Angel," he hisses. "You feel so damn good even when you're full of Shane's cum."

Shane chuckles softly as his hands slide to my hips and he rolls me gently over Conor's cock as he stares into my eyes. "Show me how you make him come, sweetheart," he growls before he looks down at my pussy being filled by his brother. Conor pulls me back against his chest, one hand around my throat and one toying with my nipple.

"Fuck, Con. She looks so damn good too," Shane hisses.

"Such a good girl," Conor growls in my ear and I whimper.

"She on the edge again already?" Shane asks as he slides his hand up my inner thigh until his fingers find my swollen clit and he begins to rub slowly.

"Shane!" I groan, and Conor tugs hard on my nipple while Shane chuckles.

"You still not learned your lesson, Angel? Who's inside you right now?" Conor asks, his lips brushing my ear as he squeezes my breast and drives himself harder into me, like I might have forgotten the answer to that question.

"You are," I pant.

"Exactly. So whose name do you moan?"

"Yours," I groan loudly as Shane increases the pressure on my clit and my impending orgasm threatens to overwhelm me.

Conor tilts my head back so I'm looking at him and can no

longer see Shane. But Conor isn't looking at me. He's looking right at his older brother with a wicked glint in his eye and the next thing I know, he has released his grip on me and begins lifting me off his cock.

"Turn around, Angel," he says softly. "I want to see your face."

I do as he tells me, shifting myself around so that I'm straddling him and looking into his handsome face. As he places his hands on my hips, he kisses me deeply before pulling me down and impaling me onto his cock and I groan into his mouth.

"Tell me who gets to fuck you whenever they want, Jessie?" he growls as he breaks our kiss.

"You do," I pant.

"And who else?"

"Shane, Mikey and Liam," I breathe as his hands slide onto my ass.

"No one else. Ever!" he growls.

"Okay."

"Damn, you're so fucking close, Angel," he hisses in my ear. "I love filling you with my cock. How about you, Shane?"

"My favorite fucking thing in the world," he replies behind me as his fingers slide down the seam of my ass. "And seeing you fucking our girl makes me desperate to be back inside her."

His hand disappears, and the sound of his zipper opening again makes me tense. "We have no lube," I breathe.

"Who needs it?" Conor laughs softly as he slides his cock out of me and a rush of cum flows with it, making my cheeks flush with heat.

Shane pushes a finger inside me, coating it in my juices before replacing it with his cock. He leans over me as Conor wraps my pony tail around his fist, giving the two of them better access to my neck, and growls in my ear. "Plenty of lube right here, sweetheart," he whispers as he pushes deeper inside me and the waves of pleasure roll through my body. A few seconds later, he pulls out of me again and Conor thrusts himself back inside me until I moan his name.

Shane lines his cock up at the seam of my ass while Conor pulls my thighs wider apart to allow his brother easier access. Shane pushes in slowly and I inch forward instinctively, but Conor holds me in place until his brother is able to press almost all the way inside. "Oh, God," I moan loudly.

"No, just me, sweetheart," Shane whispers in my ear as he pushes his hips forward until he is buried inside me.

"Shane! Conor!" I moan at the sensation of being so full of the two of them as they start to fuck me at a delicious pace as one pulls out and the other drives into me.

"Fuck! Take it easy, Angel, or I'm going to come too soon," Conor pants as my walls squeeze around him while I teeter on the edge of oblivion. I drop my head, pressing my forehead against his chest as I try to deal with the overwhelming sensation of these two incredible men and the things they're doing to me. "Our girl sure loves being fucked by both of us," Conor growls. "She is creaming all over my cock."

"Don't come yet, Jessie. Not until we say," Shane whispers in my ear.

I bite the inside of my cheek, trying to stave off the orgasm that is bursting to be released, but Conor cups my chin in his free hand and lifts my head so that I'm forced to look at him. "You like being fucked by both of us at the same time, Angel?" he growls.

"Yes," I breathe, almost on the verge of tears.

"You want to do this more often?"

"Yes," I whimper as Shane wraps one arm around my waist, pulling me tighter to him as he fucks me harder and slides his free hand over my hip and between my thighs until he finds my swollen, throbbing clit and begins to rub firmly. While Conor drops his lips to my neck and begins to suck softly as Shane presses soft kisses along my spine.

"Please? I can't hold on," I breathe as every single nerve ending in my body sizzles with electricity and euphoria. I think I really am going to pass out when they finally let me come. "This is your show, Con," Shane says quietly.

"Hmm," Conor chuckles as he keeps on nuzzling my neck and prolonging my agony. My body starts to buck between them as their hands and mouths explore me. "You can come, Angel," Conor eventually growls and my climax bursts through me like a river breaking a dam, soaking Conor and the sofa beneath us. As my entire body trembles with my release, they press me tighter between them and go on fucking me until they each find their own a few moments later.

THIRTY

T stand at the elevator and wave Conor and the twins goodnight as they head off to work for the evening. Shane walks up behind me and slips his arms around my waist.

"So, what shall we do tonight, Hacker?" he whispers in my ear.

"What do you want to do?" I ask as I turn in his arms.

"You." He flashes his eyebrows at me.

"You did me about two hours ago. You'll have to wait until later. Or I'm not going to be able to walk."

"Later then," he says with a wink. "I wish I could take you out. As soon as we're back on track with business and I don't have to worry about Liam, I'm going to take you out for dinner."

"Out? Like on a date?" I smile at him.

"Exactly like a date," he nods as he presses his lips against my neck. "I'll take you to the fanciest restaurant in New York, and then I'm going to fuck you in the restroom, and then again in the limo on the way home."

"Is that all you ever think about?"

"When you're around me, Hacker," he groans. "You drive me to distraction."

169

"How about a swim on the roof?"

He bites on his lip. "You in a bikini..."

"I don't have a bikini." I arch an eyebrow at him. "Or a swimsuit."

"Then unless you just want to go with my plan, where I just fuck you all night, that will have to be a no."

"A workout?"

"We'll end up fucking," he shrugs.

I roll my eyes. "It's a shame we can't go out somewhere."

He sucks on his top lip as though he's deep in thought. "You still have that sexy little dress you wore to the club that night?"

My insides flutter at the memory of that night when I danced with Conor, and Shane spanked me with his belt, which was as hot as hell, but then he sent me away hot and wet and needy. "Yes, I think so anyway."

"Go get yourself ready and meet me in the dining room in an hour. Wear the dress."

I frown at him, wondering what he's got up his sleeve. Shane Ryan never fails to surprise me. "Okay," I say as I turn to walk to my room.

"Jessie," he shouts after me, and I spin around to face him.

"Wear those black heels too."

I cross my arms over my chest as though I'm annoyed, but I love it when he's bossy. "The mini dress and black heels? Is that all, Sir?"

"Yes, that's all. *Nothing* else!" He arches an eyebrow at me before a wicked grin flickers across his lips.

Goosebumps prickle along my flesh and the wet heat flushes between my thighs. He stuffs his hands into his pockets and turns around, making his way toward the kitchen and leaving me to stare after him. A hot, trembling mess.

· · ·

ONE HOUR LATER, I smooth the black minidress over my thighs as I stand at the doorway to the dining room. As instructed, I'm wearing no underwear and my black six-inch pumps. My pulse thrums against my skin as I wonder what Shane has planned for the rest of the evening. As I open the door, the delicious aroma of Italian food hits me.

The table is set for two, with a single candle in the middle. Shane is serving up pasta onto plates with his back to me.

"Did you cook?" I ask as I stride into the room.

He turns to me. "No. Cooking isn't my thing. I ordered in."

"It smells incredible," I say, walking over to the table to see the plates of pasta and a selection of fresh breads. "It looks delicious."

He places the dish onto the table and slips his arm around my waist, skimming his hand over my ass and confirming I'm following his instruction. "You look delicious," he growls before planting a soft kiss on my neck.

I lean into him as a soft moan escapes my throat, and he smiles against my skin. "Let's eat, Hacker, before I eat you," he whispers in my ear. He steps aside and pulls a chair out for me to sit in and then he sits opposite me before pouring us each a glass of champagne that I hadn't even noticed was there.

"This is all incredible. Thank you," I smile as I lift my glass to his.

"It's nothing."

"Really. You do this for all the girls?" I grin at him. "I never had you down as the romantic type, Shane Ryan."

"Eat your food, Hacker!" he warns as the hint of a smile plays on his lips.

THE FOOD IS delicious and we sit and chat about all of the mundane things we can think of before we have to confront one of the topics we've been avoiding all night, because we're having such a pleasant evening.

"So, Arizona?" he asks with an arch of one eyebrow.

"Seemed like as good a place as any," I reply with a shrug.

"I've never been."

"It was nice. We should go sometime. I could take you to Ray's bar," I laugh, imagining how out of place Shane Ryan would appear in Ray's dive bar.

"I don't think that would be a good idea." He narrows his eyes at me. "Conor told me Ray was an asshole to you, and I might have to teach him some manners if I ever ran into him."

"He was an asshole. But he gave me a job with no references or anything."

Shane rolls his eyes and shakes his head.

"What?" I frown at him.

"I'm pretty sure he took one look at your ass and got all the references he needed, sweetheart," he laughs.

"Or maybe I just seemed like a nice person and a hard work-er?" I offer.

"Well, I know you're both of those things. But I would bet my life on Ray being more interested in the fact that you don't need no belt to hold up your jeans," he flashes his eyebrows at me.

"You're an asshole!" I grin at him. "Are you saying I have a fat ass?"

"No! Your ass is perfect."

I try to feign a scowl but I can't even pretend to be mad at him and I smile instead.

"Conor told me you cured his fear of the dark in Ray's base-ment?" He stares at me and the flush creeps over my neck and cheeks.

"He told you about that? I thought you guys didn't discuss what we do, you know, in private?"

"We don't," he shakes his head. "He didn't tell me how. He just said you ended up locked in a basement. And now he doesn't sleep with the light on."

"Well, I'm glad I could be of help."

"You're good for him, Hacker," he says and my heart swells with pride. "You're good for all of us," he says in that low growl that turns my insides to molten lava. The sound vibrates through my core and suddenly I'm hyper aware of the fact I'm not wearing any panties. I cross my legs beneath the table, squeezing my thighs together, and he obviously realizes because he smiles wickedly at me.

Shane has had music playing quietly in the background all evening, and Sam Smith's *Like I Can* comes on. "I love this song," I say, feeling the need to change the subject. Too much praise makes me uncomfortable.

"You want to dance?"

"Here? With you?"

"Yes." He pushes his chair back and stands, holding his hand out to me.

I reach out and take it, and his warm fingers curl around mine as he pulls me to my feet. "Volume up!" he commands, and the music gets louder.

Shane slides his hands around my hips, slipping one on to the small of my back and the other to my ass. Wrapping my arms around his neck, I lean my face against him. Damn! He always smells so freaking good.

He is a surprisingly good dancer. He presses me closer to him as our bodies move in time to the music and his cock hardens against my abdomen as we dance. "This dress is incredible on you, Hacker," he growls as he squeezes my ass in his palm.

"Thank you."

"Do you remember what happened last time you wore it?"

His hand slides lower until he reaches the edge of the fabric before slipping beneath my dress, until his palm is resting on my bare ass cheek.

"Yes," I breathe, recalling how he spanked me with his belt and then sent me to my room with my pussy dripping wet for him.

He walks us toward the sofa. "And you snuck away this morning without waking me. And I had to wake up without this sexy, warm body in my bed," he growls.

"I'm sorry. I didn't realize you'd miss me so much." I bite my lip.

"Oh, Hacker. What have I told you about lying to me?"

"I'm not lying," I breathe.

"But how could I not miss this?" he growls, squeezing my ass hard.

"So, are you going to punish me?" I purr as the heat surges between my thighs.

"What do you think, sweetheart?" He turns, sitting on the sofa and pulling me down onto his lap so I'm lying face down with my ass in the air.

"Shane!" I stifle a giggle as he pulls my dress over the top of my thighs and my hips until it is sitting around my waist. My thighs tremble in anticipation as his strong hand skims over my bare skin.

"This is a fucking beautiful backside, Hacker," he growls as he squeezes one of my ass cheeks. Then he spanks me hard and I groan loudly as the rush of wet heat almost floors me. He delivers four more hard slaps before he dips his finger inside my pussy. "You really like my spankings, Hacker?" he growls and I whimper as a rush of my cream coats his fingers. He rubs his free hand over my reddened skin, soothing the burning before he slaps me again and pushes his finger deeper inside.

My walls squeeze him, trying to pull him deeper. "Shane," I moan out loud.

"Damn! You look so good bent over my knee. I'm going to put you over it more often." He laughs softly before he withdraws his finger from my pussy and grabs my hips, pulling me into a standing position.

I blink at him. Surely that's not it? Because I am desperate for more. He narrows his eyes at me as he stands too. "Take off the dress," he growls as his hands drop to his belt buckle. I pull it off over my head until I'm standing in just my heels and when I glance back at him, he is sliding his belt off. The sound of the leather whispering against the fabric makes my knees almost give way.

He reaches out a hand to steady me, his fingers digging into my hip as his green eyes burn into mine. "You didn't think that was it, did you, Jessie?" he smiles.

"No," I whisper.

"Good," he growls as he turns me around and moves behind me, pulling my hair to one side and pressing his lips against my ear. "You're going to want to hold on to the back of the sofa, sweetheart." He keeps one hand on my hip while he places the other between my shoulder blades, forcing me to lean over the sofa. I plant my hands on the back and lock out my arms as he peppers kisses along my back and shoulders before he speaks again. "Because I'm going to make this hurt."

Those words send shivers of excitement and anticipation skittering up my spine, and I draw in a breath as my fingers flex on the sofa cushions, gripping them harder as I brace myself. I close my eyes at the sound of the leather slicing through the air before it lands with a crack across my ass cheeks. It stings like hell, but it sends more shudders of pleasure through me. He strikes me again, and a growl rumbles in his throat as my body shudders.

"Your ass looks incredible with my belt striping it, Hacker," he groans before he delivers the third blow, which hits me exactly where the last one did, as does the fourth. Damn! He knows what he's doing. The tears prick at my eyes from the sting of the burning on my skin, but I take a deep breath and wait for the next one as wetness drips down my thighs. Because I love this, and he knows it.

The next blow lands lower, at the top of my thighs, grazing my dripping pussy and I flinch, but he doesn't stop. He pushes me to the very edge of my limit, as skilled at causing pain as he is at giving pleasure. And just as I am wondering if I have the words to tell him that I've had enough, he drops the belt to the floor and his warm, rough hands run over my ass and thighs, soothing the burning as I arch my back in pleasure. "Beautiful," he growls before he sits on the sofa, pulling me to straddle him before he unzips his fly. Looking up at my face, he rubs the tears from my cheeks with the pads of his thumbs.

"I'm not crying," I whisper. "My eyes are watering."

"I know." He leans forward and plants a soft kiss on my forehead. "Now, show me how much you love my belt."

I take hold of his stiff cock and lower myself onto it, savoring the feeling of him filling me completely and letting out a low moan.

"Jesus, Hacker!" he sucks in a breath. "You feel so fucking good." He palms my ass and squeezes, making me groan wantonly. "You like that spanking?" he growls as he nuzzles my neck. "Because you're fucking soaking."

"You know I did," I moan as I roll my hips over him.

"Such a good girl," he chuckles before he bends his head lower and sucks one of my pebbled nipples into his mouth as he starts to move my hips for me. I might be on top, but there is no doubting he is in full control, pushing against the sweet spot deep inside me as his teeth graze over my skin.

"Shane," I whimper as my orgasm threatens to burst out of me at any moment.

"Let go, Jessie. I've got you," he murmurs against me and I throw my head back and obey him. Like I always do.

AFTER HE FUCKED me on the sofa, Shane carried me to his bed and ordered me to lie on my front while he disappeared into the bathroom. I lie waiting for him, with my bare ass on fire, and a few seconds later, he walks back toward the bed holding a small bottle in his hand. Sitting beside me, he pours a small amount of liquid onto his palms and rubs them together before he bends down and plants a kiss on each of my ass cheeks. Then he begins massaging them softly.

"Oh," I groan in pleasure as I press my ass into his hands. "What is that?"

"Arnica oil. It's good for bruising."

"Have you bruised my ass, Shane Ryan?" I sigh contentedly.

"No, but this will help with any swelling too."

"Well, it feels good."

"Hmm. It does," he laughs. "Your ass is incredible, Jessie."

He pushes himself off the bed, and undresses and I watch him, unapologetically staring. "Your entire body is pretty incredible," I breathe, and he smiles at me.

"You like?"

"You know that I do." I roll my eyes.

He slides onto the bed beside me. "You didn't just roll your eyes at me, did you, Hacker?" he says as he pulls me into his arms, so I'm lying on his hard chest.

"Sorry," I whisper. "You bring out the spoiled brat in me."

He runs a hand up my back and wraps my hair around his fist, tilting my head so I'm looking directly into his green eyes.

"I doubt that you were ever a spoiled brat. But, I love that you are one for me."

"You might be right. It must be your incredible spankings. I don't think anyone else brings out my bad attitude quite like you do," I giggle.

"Promise me they never will, Jessie," he whispers.

"Shane Ryan, are you telling me you enjoy me giving you attitude?"

"Well, I certainly enjoy fucking it out of you," he growls as tightens his grip on my hair and tips my head back further. "Now tell me that it's just for me."

"It's only for you, Shane," I breathe just before he presses his lips against mine and kisses me so deeply, I feel tears welling in my eyes. This closeness between us has been hard won, but it's exactly what I've always wanted from him.

With my head on Shane's chest and his arms wrapped around me, I fight the urge to sleep. He trails his fingertips up and down my back as I snuggle against him and sigh with contentment.

"You tired, Hacker?" he asks softly.

"Yes. But I don't want to go to sleep yet. I just want to lie here like this for a while. Is that okay?"

"Yeah," he whispers as his hand slips lower and he rubs it gently over my ass. "How is this beautiful ass doing?"

"It's throbbing like it has its own pulse," I giggle. "But I really like it. I'm good."

"Good." He places a kiss on the top of my head.

"How did you know just how far to go? I mean, you stopped at exactly the right time. How did you do that?"

"I understand how to test people's limits, that's all. And I know you better than you think."

"Hmm." I press my cheek against his chest and listen to the

sound of his steady heartbeat. "I wish that I understood you, Shane."

"You do. Much better than you think too, sweetheart. You've been under my skin since that day I found you in Nikolai's office and you squared up to me, even when Conor had a gun pointed in your face."

I lift my head up to look into his deep green eyes. "I have?"

"Surely you know that already? I can barely keep my fucking hands off you, Jessie. I think about you constantly. Why do you think it hurt me so much when you walked out on us and left us that damn note?"

A wave of guilt washes over me as I recall leaving a few months earlier with the man I thought was my father, and with only a brief note in my place. "I'm truly sorry that I hurt you all," I whisper.

He narrows his eyes at me and cups my chin with his hand. "I know. I'm sorry I hurt you too. But I need you to promise me you'll never leave us again. And I need you to mean it this time. I don't care who turns up here looking for you. You come talk to us about it, okay?"

"Yes. I promise."

THIRTY-ONE

LIAM

The sound of Mikey coming into the room at 6am wakes me and I sit up and blink at him. I worked until midnight in the club last night, same as I did the night before. It's felt good to be able to do something. Even if I do suspect it was something that someone else usually does for Conor anyway, but I appreciate him finding me something to do to help me feel useful.

I don't take as many pain meds now and I'm no longer sleeping for sixteen hours a day. It means I'm recovering, but it also means I have much more time on my hands. I'm not a big reader, and I think I've watched every good program Netflix has to offer. And now that Shane is back, and Conor isn't working so much, I no longer have my hot nurse mostly to myself to spend the whole day and night with me. I miss waking up with her next to me.

Mikey flops into bed with exhaustion while I suddenly am wide awake. I climb out of bed and wander down the quiet hallway. Everyone is sleeping and I feel a sense of loneliness being the only person up and about.

I make my way to the stairway leading to the roof and head

up to the terrace. It's a beautiful space, and we don't use it nearly often enough. The morning is warm and the sun is coming up. I tilt my face toward it and let the sunlight warm my skin. The sound of the street below reminds me that I'm not alone. Despite the occupants of our apartment sleeping, the city is very much awake.

I lean on the railing, looking at the streets coming to life below and have no idea how long I stay there before I hear footsteps behind me. Turning around, I see Jessie walking toward me.

"Good morning. You're up early," she says with a smile as she reaches me and slides her warm arm around my waist.

"I couldn't sleep." I kiss her head and wrap my arm around her shoulder. "How did you know I was up here?"

"I came to see if you needed anything and you weren't in bed. And you weren't in the apartment, and I saw the door to the roof open."

"You should be a detective," I chuckle, and she rolls her eyes and smiles up at me.

"This is some view," she says as she peers over the railing.

"Sure is."

"You feel cold."

"I'm fine," I say with a sigh.

"I'm not nagging you," she whispers. "I just worry about you."

"I know, baby. But I promise, I'm fine. It's nice to get some fresh air. Are you cold?"

"A little," she shivers.

I turn around and wrap my arms around her. "Come with me and I'll keep you warm," I whisper in her ear before we walk to the pool and the sun loungers. We have towels in a locker up here, and I take one out and wrap it around her shoulders.

"Thank…" she starts to say, but then she looks over my shoulder and her flushed cheeks suddenly turn pale.

I turn around to see what it is that has spooked her.

"What's that in the pool, Liam?" she whispers.

I blink at the small, dark mass in the pool. We usually have it covered, but I've been swimming up here the past few days because it's good for my recovery. "It's a dead bird, baby. That's all. I'll fish it out later."

"Is it a Blue Jay?" she asks with a tremor in her voice.

I release her from my embrace and walk closer to the pool and she follows a few steps behind me. "I think so. Why?"

"There's blood."

"Yeah," I agree as a small pool of blood surrounds the bird. "We'll get the pool cleaned." I turn to her and frown and her entire body is trembling from head to toe and she is so pale, I'm worried she's going to pass out.

"Jessie." I walk back to her, wrapping her in my arms again and holding her close to me. "What is it, baby?"

"Do you get many Blue Jays dead on your roof?"

I look down at her. "Not really. But this is New York. There are birds everywhere. I'm pretty sure we've had a few dead ones up here before. It probably drowned in the pool or something."

"But it was bleeding." She shivers in my arms.

"So?"

"So, like someone hurt it. And then they put it here."

"We're ten floors up, Jessie. It fell out of the sky. Maybe someone shot it and it flew away?" I look down at her and the sickening feeling in the pit of my stomach begins to grow. This isn't about a dead bird.

I walk us over to a sun lounger and sit down, pulling her onto my lap. I brush the hair back from her pale face. "What is it? It's just a bird."

"No. It's a Blue Jay," she stammers.

I frown at her as she stares into the distance.

"Jessie. I need you to tell me what's going on, baby. Because you're freaking me out."

She turns and looks at me. "Sorry," she says with a shake of her head, as though she has come back to reality.

"Don't be sorry. Just tell me what's wrong?"

She swallows hard and nods her head, but it's a few seconds before she speaks. "When the Wolf kept me prisoner, I had no one to talk to. I never saw another living soul the whole time I was there. He didn't like animals, and he used to shoot the raccoons or the birds that came into the yard. It was like a sport. He would lie on the roof with his sniper rifle and pick them off," she shudders and I pull her closer. "One day, I found an injured Blue Jay. I made it a nest from branches and leaves and I nursed it back to health. I understood that as soon as it could fly, it would leave the yard, and I wanted it to, because he would have shot it anyway. So, I knew that I was never going to keep it. But for two weeks, I cared for it every day and I lived for my hour outside where I could check on it and make sure it was okay. It was so nice just to have another heartbeat around, you know?" She wipes a tear from her eye and I swear my heart is about to break into pieces. "It was doing really well. It was almost ready to fly, and then one morning I woke up and it was on the pillow next to me."

"Jessie." I squeeze her tighter.

"He had sliced off its head, and left it there with blood dripping onto my sheets." She wipes her cheeks again as the tears run down them.

I pull her against my chest, and she sobs in my arms. While I hold her there, I look at the bird in the pool. It still has its head. No doubt, it was shot or injured and it flew up here and died. But my girl is spooked and I can't blame her after what she just told me.

When she stops crying, she looks up at me and I wipe the tears from her face with the towel. "You okay?"

"Yes," she nods. "You think it did just fly up here and die, Liam?"

"Yes. New York is full of Blue Jays, baby."

"I know," she sniffs.

"I'll get Mikey to fish it out and we'll bury it somewhere. Okay?"

"Okay," she says as she lays back against me. "I'm sorry for being such a crazy person."

"You are not crazy. Not even a little bit," I assure her. "I'm sorry for everything he did to you, Jessie. If I ever meet him, I will happily cut his head off for you."

"Thank you," she says and I see the hint of a smile on her lips before she cuddles closer to my chest.

I wince instinctively as she shifts her position and she gasps out loud, sitting up quickly. "I'm sorry, Liam. Your ribs." She bites her lip.

"My ribs are good. Come back here." I hold my arms out. "Now!"

"When did you boys all get so bossy?" she says as she leans back against me.

I cup her chin in my hand and tilt her face up so I can look into her bright blue eyes. "You haven't even seen me bossy yet," I grin at her and she smiles back up at me so fucking genuinely that it makes me want to bury myself in her. I lean down and kiss her softly and she melts into me, deepening our kiss and allowing me to slide my tongue into her mouth. She tastes of peppermint and coffee and I have to hold myself back from flipping her over and nailing her to this sun lounger because she just damn near passed out from terror at the sight of a dead bird and the memories it triggered.

But she slides her hand from beneath the towel and onto

my bare stomach, trailing it down to the band of my sweatpants before slipping her hand inside and squeezing my cock, which was already stiffening and it completely hardens in her hand.

"You want that, baby?" I ask her as she squeezes harder.

"Yes," she pants.

I pull her up and she swings her legs around until she is straddling me. "Show me," I groan as I press soft kisses against the sweet smelling skin on her throat. She works my pants down so my cock is free and rubs the pad of her thumb across the tip, making my balls draw up into my stomach.

My hands dip beneath her t-shirt until I find her panties, pushing my hand inside until my fingers slide over her wet clit and her soft moan rumbles in her throat. She works my cock, pumping the shaft as I slide my fingers lower until I find her slick heat and push two fingers deep inside her and she coats me in her juices.

"You're so fucking wet, baby," I growl in her ear and she lets go of my cock, wrapping her arms around my neck instead, she whimpers as I fuck her with my fingers until her cum is running down my hand and onto my wrist.

"God, Liam," she groans and my dick throbs at the sound as her walls squeeze around me. She rocks her hips as she presses her face against my neck and comes hard for me.

When she's stopped trembling, I pull my fingers out of her and tug her panties to the side. "Slide that hot pussy onto my cock, Jessie."

She looks at me as she does as she's told, licking her lips as she lowers herself onto me. Her eyes roll when she is all the way down and I pull her deeper as her pussy clenches and releases around me. "You're so hot and tight, baby," I hiss as she drives me crazy with her hungry squeezes. "Do you have any idea how much I missed this pussy when you left us?"

"Liam." Her cheeks flush pink and she buries her head in my

neck again as I wrap my arms around her and hold her to me while she rides my cock like a pro.

"You'll never keep it from me again, will you?" I growl in her ear as I get so close to the edge, I'm about to fall into oblivion with her. This girl is my whole fucking world.

"No," she breathes as she holds onto me and I come inside her with a roar that I'm pretty sure could be heard on the street below. I slip my hand between us and rub her clit as she keeps on rolling her hips over my cock, chasing her second orgasm, which hits a few seconds later.

I press my forehead against hers. "That is the most fun I have ever had on this rooftop," I grin at her.

"It's the most fun I've ever had on any rooftop," she giggles, slightly breathless from our exertions. I brush the hair back from her face, glad to see her happy again and recovered from the whole Blue Jay incident. But that doesn't mean I'm still not freaked out, and will be speaking to my brothers about it as soon as I get the chance.

THIRTY-TWO

JESSIE

I took an extra long soak in the tub after Liam and I came down from the roof. Seeing that Blue Jay dead in the pool brought back so many buried memories. I wonder if I will ever be free of my past and the hold that the Wolf still has over me. But Liam was right. New York City is full of birds and while it's not common to find a dead one in the pool, it's not unlikely either. The poor thing must have been injured and fallen onto the roof.

At least that's what I keep telling myself, despite my mind trying to convince me otherwise.

I slather my body in my favorite vanilla body butter and pull on a clean t-shirt and panties before going to find the brothers.

I check the kitchen and the den first, but they are empty. Liam said he was going back to bed, and I expect Conor and Mikey will still be sleeping too, so I walk along to Shane's office to see if he's awake, because he's likely to be in there. The door to his office is open and I pop my head inside, surprised to see all four Ryan brothers in there with serious looks on their faces. Mikey and Conor are only wearing shorts and look like they've just got out of bed and I can't help but wonder why they appear to be having a family meeting without me.

"Jessie," Shane says as he looks up and sees me and the other three turn their heads and look at me too.

"What's going on?" I stammer as I step inside the room, with the distinct impression that I am missing something.

Conor holds out a hand to me. "Come on in, Angel."

I take his hand and he pulls me to sit on the sofa between him and Liam.

"I was just telling them about the bird," Liam says. "In the pool."

I blink at him, and then I look at their concerned faces. "But you said it was just a bird. Nothing to worry about."

"Of course it was," Liam replies, taking my hand and squeezing it gently.

"Yeah. We've found at least half a dozen dead birds on that roof," Conor adds.

"So why are you all sitting here talking about me? Like I'm crazy or something?" I hear my voice going up a few octaves, but I can't stop the panic and hysteria from setting in again. Liam convinced me it was nothing, and now they're all looking at me like it's something.

"Liam just wanted us to know what happened, is all." Conor reaches for my hand, but I snatch it away, pulling my other hand from Liam's at the same time.

"Did you all have a good laugh at how crazy I am freaking out about a dead bird?" I say, spiraling into some sort of panic attack meltdown that I can't seem to stop.

"No, Jessie," Liam shakes his head.

"Really? You expect me to believe that?" I push myself up and start to walk out of the room.

"Jessie Ryan!" Shane shouts at me in a tone that makes me

freeze in my tracks, and I turn to look at him. "Sit your ass back down."

I glance back at Liam and Conor who avert their eyes while Mikey clears his throat nervously.

"Now!" Shane barks, and I hesitate for a few seconds before I walk back to the sofa and take my seat again.

"Look at me," Shane growls and I lift my head to see him glaring at me. "You want to think about what you just said?"

I swallow as I glare back at him. "I'm sorry. I know you wouldn't do that."

He runs a tongue along his lip and then sits back in his chair, seemingly satisfied with my response. "Yes, we were talking about you, but of course we weren't laughing at you. Because if there is *any* possibility that you are in danger, Jessie, then we will talk about it. Conor was about to come and get you so we could discuss it with you too before you walked in here."

"Oh?" I swallow. "I'm sorry. But the Wolf, he..." I shake my head. "He gets under my skin. I feel like I go crazy whenever I think about him."

Conor takes my hand again and I curl my fingers around his just as Liam reaches for my other hand and I lean back in my seat, feeling comfort from the warmth of their bodies.

"Well, that's understandable given everything you went through, baby," Liam says quietly.

"Yeah, Red," Mikey agrees.

"Do you think it was him then?" I ask.

"No," they all say in unison.

"Just a dead bird, Angel," Conor adds softly. "Me and Mikey scooped it out of the pool and there was nothing suspicious."

I nod, chewing on my lip absent-mindedly. "I'm sorry I said those things," I say again.

"You already apologized twice," Shane says with a soft sigh.

"I know," I say with a shake of my head. "But I feel bad for accusing you all like that."

"Jessie," Shane sighs as he stands up from his desk and walks across the room. "We're family, right?"

"Yes."

"So, that means you get to say pretty much anything you want when you're upset, and we'll get over it," he smiles at me.

"Yep," Mikey nods. "And we know better than anyone how your past can fuck you up, Red. We got more skeletons in our closets than Calvary Cemetery."

"Yeah? But you guys don't freak out when you see a dead bird on the roof." I arch an eyebrow.

"You didn't freak out, baby," Liam assures me. "And you are not the only person in this room who lets their past get to them occasionally."

"Yep," Conor nods. "We're all fucked up here. That's why you fit in so well." He winks at me and I smile at him. God, I love him so much.

"Tell her why we left Ireland, Shane," Liam says softly.

Shane looks between Mikey and Liam. "You sure?" he frowns.

"Yeah," they both say.

"Okay," he says, pulling over a chair and taking a seat in front of the sofa. "Conor told you that he was a bare-knuckle boxing champion, right?"

"Yes," I nod.

"Well, Liam and Mikey used to fight too." He looks between the two of them again and they nod for him to go on. "Well, back in Ireland, my father was often involved in these under-ground fights, where basically the two fighters would fight to the death."

I open my mouth in horror. "He made Mikey and Liam do that?"

Shane runs his tongue over his lip and sucks in a deep

breath. "Yes. But that's not it. You have to understand that the fighters in these matches didn't really have much choice, Jessie. Who the hell wants to go into a fight knowing there's a fifty percent chance you won't make it out alive?"

Conor shifts beside me and Liam starts taking deep breaths and I hold his hand tighter. "So, what happened if they refused to fight?" I ask.

"Then they would face a very angry crowd who paid a lot of money to watch two guys beat the shit out of each other, and they would both get torn apart instead."

I swallow the bile as it burns the back of my throat. "That is so brutal."

"Yeah," Shane nods. "And Patrick Ryan entered his youngest sons in a competition. Against each other."

"What?" My hand instinctively flies to my mouth. "So he expected them to fight? For one of them to kill the other?"

"Yeah," Conor says.

"What happened?" I ask, looking between the four of them.

"It was fucking carnage," Mikey says with a haunted expression on his face as Liam simply nods. "Obviously, we refused to fight each other. I begged that bastard to get us out of there. Both of us offered to fight anyone else if he would let the other go, but that sick fuck wouldn't even consider it. And when we wouldn't fight each other, that vicious cunt fed us to a baying mob."

Liam shudders beside me and Mikey sits on the desk with a scowl on his face.

"It was fucking awful," Liam sucks in a shaky breath. "Hands pulling at us and feet stomping on our heads. They were trying to tear us apart. Like we were animals and not even people."

"How did you get out of there?" I whisper as my heart physically hurts at the thought of what they went through. And if it was just before they came to New York, they must have only been sixteen.

Mikey and Liam don't answer, so Shane continues for them. "Conor and I found out about our father's lunatic plan and we got there just in time to get them out."

"They were in such a bad way," Conor adds. "We thought we were going to lose them. Liam almost died on the operating table in the hospital."

"And that's why we hate hospitals." Mikey arches an eyebrow at me.

"And that's why you left Ireland?"

"Yeah," Liam says softly. "We were on a plane two days later. Mikey and I could barely walk but Shane and Conor practically carried us onto that plane."

"It probably wasn't even the worst thing he ever did to us," Mikey says with a shake of his head. "But it was the look on his face when he saw how fucking terrified we were. I have never seen that sadistic cunt look at me with so much happiness in his eyes."

"He sounds like a maniac." I shake my head, trying to comprehend how someone could do that to his own children.

"He is. Which is why we've never spoken to the evil bastard since," Mikey snarls.

"I'm so sorry that you went through that." I swallow hard as the four Ryan brothers sit in silence, and I feel the need to lighten the mood. "Jeez! And I thought my father was a psychopath."

Liam turns to me and smiles. "Erm. He definitely was, baby. Patrick Ryan and Alexei Ivanov are both up there."

"I guess so."

"All this talk of Ireland makes me want to lie down in a dark room," Mikey says as he stands up. "Are we done here?"

"Are we?" Shane looks at me.

"If you're all sure that there was no one on our roof, then yes, I don't think there's anything left to discuss."

"Good. I need me some sleep." Mikey stretches and yawns.

"I need to lie down," Liam groans as he lets go of my hand before standing up and flexes his shoulders.

"You mind if I keep you both company?" I ask.

"I was counting on it," Liam winks at me and Mikey nods his agreement.

Conor and Shane get up from their seats and each give me a soft kiss on the cheek before I walk out of Shane's office with the twins.

Ten minutes later, I'm lying in Liam's bed, sandwiched between him and Mikey as the three of us watch TV. Mikey traces his fingertips up and down my forearm, his eyelids flickering as he fights sleep, while Liam holds my hand and rubs the pad of his thumb over my knuckles.

"I love you both so much. You know that, right?" I say as we lie in silence.

"Yes, Red," Mikey mumbles sleepily. "I love you too."

"Love you, baby," Liam adds and I smile. We are all damaged by our pasts, but we are all stronger for them too. The fact that we have found a way through all of our trauma and the betrayals of the past few months to be here right now, makes me happier than I had ever dreamed possible. I have held onto my thirst for revenge for so long, and maybe now is the time to let it go.

I thought that the Wolf took everything from me, but he can't take my present or my future. Not unless I allow him to. And I won't. This life is mine and I will fight for it with every breath in my body. But perhaps it's time to let the ghost of the Wolf go.

THIRTY-THREE
CONOR

I watch Jessie and my younger brothers walking out of Shane's office and smile at the way she always knows exactly what each of us need. Despite reliving her own trauma today, she is there for them now when they need her, and they didn't even have to ask.

The night Shane and I pulled our younger brothers out of the middle of that crowd, who were determined to have their blood, still gives me nightmares. They were just kids, and they were being tossed around like pieces of meat, as though they weren't even human at all. I have killed plenty of people in my lifetime, at least three men at that fight that night, but I have never seen such blatant disregard for human life than from the mob of *respectable* everyday men who almost tore my sixteen year old brothers to pieces.

Shane played it down for Jessie's and my brother's sake, but that night was terrifying. None of us like to talk about it because it was the scariest night of our whole damn lives. Shane and I were lucky to get out alive ourselves. We all bear the scars. Patrick Ryan pulled some twisted shit with all of us when we were kids, but that was a whole new level.

"You think they're all okay?" Shane asks as he steps up behind me.

"Yeah. A morning of TV and whatever else in bed with Jessie and they'll be just fine."

"Hmm," he mumbles. "So tell me more about this Blue Jay on the roof?"

"Mikey fished it out. It looked like it had been shot by an air rifle or some kind of pellet gun. Probably flew as far as it could and fell into the pool," I shrug.

"You don't think it was planted up there by anyone then?" he frowns at me.

"I think we'd know if someone had been on our roof terrace, Shane. But, even so, it looks like it was just one of those things. Unsurprisingly, it freaked our girl out though."

"Yeah," he nods as he rubs a hand over his jaw. "But not knowing who the Wolf is makes me nervous, Con. He could be anyone."

"It makes me nervous too, bro. But I don't know what else we do to find him?"

Shane sits at his desk and opens up his laptop. "Did I tell you I had a call from good old uncle Paul while you were in Arizona?"

"Pol?" I frown at him. "Fuck, Shane. We haven't heard from him for over twenty years. Why didn't you tell me?"

"With everything else that's been going on, it slipped my mind, Con."

"How did he get in touch with you? Where the hell has he been?"

"It was my business number. No idea where he's been. But he said he'd heard a rumor the Wolf had surfaced in Russia. I pressed him for more, but he warned me to back off."

"You think he knows who the Wolf is?"

"Nobody knows who he is, Con. No one except Jessie,

anyway. But maybe Pol has some information that could give us a lead, at least?"

"You know how to get in touch with him?"

Shane shakes his head. "Nope. As elusive as ever. But he said he'd be at the funeral when that evil fucker finally dies. I'll ply the old bastard with a few whiskies and find out whatever he knows."

"If he knows anything at all. It seems like the Wolf is a ghost, Shane. He could be dead for all we know."

"I know, Con. But I don't think Jessie will ever feel safe unless she knows one way or the other. Do you?"

"No," I agree with him.

"Why don't you go check on them and get some sleep? You look exhausted."

"Yeah. I will. Catch you later, bro."

"Later," he winks at me and I leave his office and go to find Jessie and the twins.

I find them in Liam's bed, watching TV. "You guys okay?" I ask as I sit on the edge of the bed.

"Yeah, bro," the twins mumble.

"Yes," Jessie smiles sweetly and holds her arms out to me. Unable to resist an invitation to be anywhere near her hot body, I crawl onto the bed and she spreads her legs wide so I can lie between them, with my head resting on her stomach. She runs her fingers through my hair and the four of us lie there in silence and I feel so comfortable and content that I fall asleep.

THIRTY-FOUR

CONOR

I pull Jessie onto my lap as Mikey places two bowls of popcorn on the coffee table in front of us before sitting beside us on the sofa. A few seconds later, Liam sits beside him and Jessie stretches her legs out across Mikey's until her toes are almost touching Liam's thigh, and he bends his head and kisses them softly, making her squirm and giggle The sound of her laughing is so fucking good to hear.

Mikey and Liam smile at her and she leans against my chest, her cheeks flushed pink. She looks up as Shane walks into the room and I wait for the change in her, for the tension to slip into her body, but it doesn't. She stays relaxed, even as he reaches us and stands there with a frown on his face.

"No room for me then?" he asks with an arch of one eyebrow.

"You snooze, you lose, bro," Liam laughs and Mikey grins up at him.

Shane, my grumpy big brother, who never takes a night off work to watch a movie with us, simply rolls his eyes before leaning down and kissing Jessie softly before taking a seat on the nearby armchair. It has been a week since he got back from his business trip and things finally seem back to normal around here. In fact, I have never seen my brothers happier.

"Hey, I meant to tell you, Con, I found out what kept blocking up the garbage disposal. It was a piece of Cyril's ear," Mikey laughs as he tosses some popcorn into his mouth.

Jessie looks between the two of us with an expression of horror on her face. "You put someone's ear in the garbage disposal?"

"No, Angel," I tell her, brushing her hair back from her face. "At least not up here in the apartment, anyway."

"So who is Cyril?" she frowns as she looks between the four of us.

Shane flashes his eyebrows at me while Liam and Mikey glance at each other. The truth is none of us want us to think about Cyril and what happened to him.

"What is it? Who, or what, is Cyril?" she asks again, her voice going up a few octaves as she shifts on my lap.

"Cyril was a teddy bear," I say with a sigh.

"A teddy bear?" She rolls her lips together as though she's trying to stop herself from laughing. "Who did he belong to?"

I look at my brothers, and they stare back at me. "What?" Jessie says, the edge creeping into her voice as the four of us share uneasy glances.

"Cyril was a huge teddy bear that Conor bought for you the day you left with Alexei Ivanov," Shane answers her question.

"Oh?" she says and I sigh inwardly as the change in her demeanor is instant.

"He was as big as you, Jessie," Liam adds.

"What happened to him?" She turns to me, her eyes wide and brimming with tears.

There are a few second's silence and I wonder who is going to answer because she is fucking killing me here.

"Conor tore him to pieces after you left and set him on fire. Most of him anyway," Mikey eventually answers.

A single tear runs down her face and I brush it away with the pad of my thumb. I know that she still feels so much guilt for what happened that day, even though we all understand why she did what she did. And we have all forgiven her, but I don't think she has forgiven herself.

That day when she left almost broke me. It almost broke all of us. It's still too painful to think about, and it makes me feel sick whenever I do. It still stings like fuck. And now the memory of it is here in the room with the five of us, like someone who has gate-crashed our movie night. And while Jessie and I talked about her leaving during our drive back from Arizona, I'm pretty sure the rest of my brothers have avoided discussing it too much because it just fucking hurts. I see the pain in Jessie's eyes too and wish I could take it away for her.

"I'm so sorry," she says as a sob catches in her throat. "Cyril sounds lovely."

"He wasn't. He was the ugliest bear I've ever seen," I tell her. "He deserved to die a terrible death."

"Stop trying to make me feel better," she sniffs. "I can't believe you bought me a teddy bear."

"It truly was fucking hideous, Jessie," Mikey says as he takes her hand in his.

"I know you're only being nice," she says with a shake of her head. "I don't know what I can do to make it up to all of you."

We all sit in silence as the atmosphere in the room grows increasingly tense. Damn Cyril! It's Shane who eventually breaks the tension as he stands and walks over to us. Cupping Jessie's chin in his hand, he tilts her head so she can look up at him. "You want to be punished for leaving us, sweetheart? Will that make you feel better?" He narrows his eyes at her.

"Yes," she breathes, taking me by surprise.

"If we do this, then we move on. No more guilt. No more feeling bad every time that day is mentioned, okay?"

"Okay," she nods.

Shane licks his lips and then his eyes flicker to mine for a moment and I am left wondering what the hell he is cooking up in that devious mind of his. "Go to your room," he nods toward the hallway. "We'll be along in a little while, just as soon as we've figured out what your punishment is going to be," he orders.

I release her from my embrace and she stands obediently, with her head slightly bowed. I've never wanted to do the whole punishment thing with her because what we have is about something much deeper than I've ever experienced before. But fuck me if seeing her submissive side doesn't make me as hard as fucking iron.

"Okay," she whispers before she heads out of the room, leaving Liam, Mikey and me to stare up at our oldest brother and wait for him to explain what kind of punishment he's thinking about. The wicked glint in his eyes tells me it won't be about punishment at all.

THIRTY-FIVE
JESSIE

As the minutes slowly drag by, I become increasingly anxious about whatever the Ryan brothers are concocting in the other room. The truth is, I do want to be punished for leaving them. Maybe then I could stop hating myself so much for it. I could stop imagining the pain they must have gone through when they realized I'd walked out on them after promising I would never leave. But now I'm sitting here on my bed, wondering what the hell I've let myself in for.

When the door opens a few moments later, I look up expectantly to see the four men I love more than anything in the world, walking into the room, each dressed in only sweatpants except for Shane who wears his suit pants and his belt, and all looking hotter than molten lava.

My entire body trembles from head to toe as I watch them saunter toward me, oozing sex and swagger.

Damn! I think my ovaries just exploded.

Mikey carries an ice bucket with champagne inside and he sets it down on the nightstand, while Conor holds something black in his hands. As he gets closer, I see that it's my scarf and gloves from the rack in the hallway. Liam sits on the edge of the bed beside me and as he does I see the bottle of lube he's holding. Holy fuck!

"Get her naked. Now!" Shane barks to Mikey and Liam, who dutifully oblige. Liam turns to me and pulls his t-shirt over my head, while Mikey kneels in front of me and hooks his fingers into the waistband of my panties, before pulling them down quickly and stuffing them into the pocket of his pants. Within five seconds, I am completely naked while the four of them surround me.

Conor holds out the gloves to me. "Put these on, Angel," he growls.

"Why?" I whisper, looking between the gloves in his outstretched hand and his eyes which sparkle wickedly.

"We want to make it as hard as possible for you to identify who is doing what to you," he grins at me. "The less you can feel with your hands, the better."

"We were going to tie you up, but we need you to be able to move around," Shane adds and a shiver of excitement laced with fear skitters up my spine.

I take the gloves and pull the soft leather over my fingers. They were a gift from the brothers and cost more than a month's rent on my apartment in Arizona, and they fit me like a second skin.

When I have them on, Conor leans forward with my cashmere scarf. "For your eyes, Angel," he growls, and I bow my head slightly, allowing him to blindfold me. I suppress a smile as I think about how it is going to take a lot more than this for me not to recognize my boys.

"Lie on the bed, baby," Liam says once I'm blindfolded. I move back, feeling my way into the middle and then I lie there waiting for whatever punishment they are about to dole out to me, although in my mind all I can think about is this seems much more like pleasure. They could have bound me completely and I would fear nothing from any of them, and that realization makes me so happy I could almost purr.

"You ready for your punishment, Hacker?" Shane growls.

"Yes," I breathe as I lie waiting.

"You don't get to come until we say you can, okay?"

"Yes."

"And from now on, you don't speak. Unless it's to say our names, or the words, yes and no. You got that?" he adds.

"Yes," I am almost panting now. I feel the heat and the energy from their bodies as I lie there waiting for them to touch me. Being unable to see heightens my other senses, and I can smell Shane's cologne. The expensive soap that Conor uses. The oil from the car that Mikey was tinkering with just before he came upstairs. And the ointment I've been rubbing on Liam's wounds to make sure they heal as fast as possible.

I hear them moving around, but they don't speak. Then I hear the sound of the ice in the bucket moving when the champagne is taken out, followed a few seconds later by the foil being removed. When the loud pop of the cork happens a moment later, I don't flinch because I was expecting it.

"Hold onto the pillow, and do not move those hands unless you're told you can, Angel," Conor growls and I nod my compliance as I reach back and grab the pillow beneath my head.

"Now, spread those legs, Jessie," Shane orders and once again I do as I'm told before a few seconds later, the bed dips in front of me and I feel two rough hands running from my ankles to my thighs. I would know those hands anywhere, but even if I didn't, I would be able to identify who this was, because he can never resist running the pad of his thumb over the scar on the inside of my thigh.

"Mikey," I groan as his fingers brush over my folds and he chuckles softly.

"That's right, Red," he says before he slides one finger deep inside me and I arch my back in pleasure as I feel another body to the left of me.

"Liam," I say his name softly as he was sitting on the bed beside me and I didn't feel him move.

"We're going to have to make this harder, baby," Liam says against my ear before he begins trailing soft kisses over my neck and down to my breasts, before sucking one of my pebbled nipples into his mouth at the same time that Mikey does the same to my clit and my hips almost shoot off the bed.

As I'm trying to focus on the maddening teasing of the twins' hot mouths, the bed to the right side of me dips and I brace myself for another mouth, but instead ice cold champagne falls onto the hot skin of my chest, making me gasp as it fizzes over my skin, running a trail between my breasts, pooling in my belly button and trickling down between my thighs where Mikey laps it up while he's eating my pussy.

Liam moves lower, licking up some of the expensive bubbles while another hot mouth sucks on my right nipple and I writhe in pleasure as my fingers grip the pillow tighter. The sensation of three hot mouths on me is maddening and as I'm trying to determine if the third one belongs to Conor or Shane, it disappears and I groan loudly, but it is back again a few seconds later, except this time it is ice cold as he sucks my nipple into his mouth along with the ice cube he now has in there. His teeth graze me softly and I focus on the sensation as I figure out who that sexy mouth belongs to. I want to reach out and touch them so badly, but I haven't been given permission to, and I want to do this right for them.

"Conor," I eventually breathe and I hear Shane laughing in the background, confirming I'm right.

"She's good," he says with a chuckle.

"She guessed us all. Can I make her come now?" Mikey

groans against my pussy as he keeps sucking and licking me with his amazing tongue.

"Hmm," Shane agrees. "Maybe she'll have more difficulty identifying your cocks, because she sure as hell knows your mouths."

I want to ask whether I'm going to get to feel Shane's hot mouth, or his cock, but I'm not allowed to ask questions either, so I stay quiet. Well, at least I try to as Mikey pushes two of his thick fingers inside me while he keeps nuzzling on my clit and my hips rock against him. Conor and Liam's hands hold me down as they run over my body, along with their tongues, and I swear I think I'm about to pass out.

"Oh, God!" I hiss as the waves of pleasure roll over me.

At which point Mikey stops. "I don't think 'oh' or 'god' are on the agreed list of words, Red," he says with a chuckle.

"Nope. Definitely not," Shane confirms.

"Damn! Not going to be able to let you come just yet then, Red," Mikey sighs and I groan loudly, resisting the urge to say how unfair that is.

"Mikey," I pant instead.

"Aw, Red. I would love to make you come all over my tongue. But rules is rules," he says with an overly dramatic sigh as he trails kisses along my thighs instead and a few seconds later he is gone altogether and Liam's hand is sliding between my thighs, rubbing between my folds but purposely avoiding the spot where I desperately want him as he continues to leave me teetering on the edge of oblivion.

"Liam?" I pant.

"Sorry, baby," he chuckles. "Soon, though. Be a good girl and we might let you come later."

"Hmm," Conor mumbles against my skin as trails kisses across my breast before sucking on my other nipple. I hear more rustling in the ice bucket before someone is at my front again and Liam's hand slides back up to my stomach. Whoever it is, rubs an ice cube through my folds and I buck my hips at the coldness and the contrast between that and the heat that is coursing through my body. Then he pushes it inside my opening and I gasp out loud before he drops his head and laps the melting water from my pussy.

"Fuck!" Mikey hisses, confirming it is him again. Then there are ice cubes in Conor's and Liam's hands and I realize Mikey must have handed them some and they swirl them over my stomach and breasts before licking off the melted liquid.

I writhe in pleasure as more champagne is poured over my breasts. Damn! Are all four of them here now? Or does Liam or Conor have hold of the bottle? I can't tell any longer as I teeter on the edge of an earth shattering orgasm and multiple hands and mouths devour my entire body. I can hardly focus on anything and I'm going to come, really hard.

My thighs tremble and my insides contract as the orgasm threatens to burst out of me at any moment.

"Don't you fucking dare, Hacker," Shane warns from nearby, confirming he's not on the bed with me.

"Shane?" I plead with him. I cannot hold out much longer while his brothers are torturing me with their sinful tongues and fingers. Conor's hand is traveling southwards, he circles the tip of his index finger over my clit, and I moan so loudly, I'm sure the walls of the apartment shake.

"Finish her off," Shane eventually says and at the exact same time Liam sucks my nipple and grazes it with his teeth, Mikey pushes his hot tongue inside my pussy and Conor pushes down on my clit like it is a nuclear detonator and I lose all sense of time and space. I'm not sure if that was my permission too, but I am no longer in control of my body.

My orgasm crashes over me like a full scale tsunami and my entire body trembles violently as the three of them continue to coax the last tremors from me until I am lying beneath them like a gibbering wreck. Tears are spilling over my cheeks as my senses completely overwhelm me. When it has completely subsided, I feel them moving away, but not before each pressing a soft kiss on my stomach first.

I lie there, panting and gasping for breath as I wait for the next round of delicious punishment, as I wonder what I ever did to deserve the devotion of these four incredible men.

CHAPTER
THIRTY-SIX

SHANE

I squeeze my cock through my pants as I look at our girl lying on the bed, legs spread open and her cum dripping from her pussy. She looks completely wrung out, but we've barely even started yet. Now, she gets to take all four of our cocks and it's taking all of my restraint not to bury mine in her right now. My brothers are aware of what's about to happen next and they're busy removing their sweatpants while I stare at her.

Fuck! She makes me so fucking hard. I can't resist tasting her before she's filled with my brothers' cum and I crawl between her thighs, which are still trembling. Pressing the flat of my tongue against her slit, I lick from her pussy opening to her clit and she shudders beneath me. I don't touch her anywhere else, even though I'm desperate to put my hands on her. But I suck her swollen clit into my mouth and suck her sweet juices.

"Shane," she says with a soft moan that makes my balls draw up into my stomach.

I lift my head and place my hands on her hips and my fingers dig into her soft flesh. Damn! I could eat this girl alive.

"Did you know that was me? Or was it an educated guess? I want the truth, Hacker," I growl.

She opens her mouth, but she doesn't answer and I realize it's because she is playing by the rules I set out for her earlier, and that makes me even harder. "You can answer," I tell her.

"I would know your mouth anywhere," she says with a contented smile that makes my heart feel like it's going to burst out of my chest. I think about undoing my belt, taking my cock out and driving it into her as I ask her if she would recognize that anywhere too. But, I am a patient man. Instead, I climb off the bed and I don't fail to notice her smile disappearing when I do.

"Sit up and come here, Hacker," I say to her and she pushes herself onto her knees and crawls over to me, I reach out and take her hand to guide her to the edge of the bed, until she's kneeling right in front of me. Her mouth is open in expectation and I lean down and kiss her, distracting her as Conor lies down on the bed behind her. She runs her hands over my chest, but the soft leather gloves are no substitute for the warm caress of her fingertips. I slide one hand to her ass and squeeze hard and she groans into my mouth as I deepen our kiss and take everything I can from her.

My cock is busting the zipper of my pants and I am fucking desperate to get inside her as soon as possible. When Conor is in place, I pull back from her. "Turn around, sweetheart," I whisper in her ear.

She does so without hesitation and her submissiveness is such a fucking turn on. Conor reaches up and takes her hand, guiding her toward him.

"Slide yourself onto his cock, Hacker," I tell her and she feels her way up his thighs until she finds it. I watch as she squeezes it and Conor bites his lip to stifle a groan. Then she slides her hot pussy onto him and I close my eyes as I recall how good it feels to have her cunt squeezing my cock. I'm impressed by Conor's restraint because I understand how desperate he must be to grab her by the hips or moan her fucking name.

"Now ride him, Hacker," I growl, and she presses her hands flat on his chest and starts to roll her hips over him as his eyes almost roll back in his head.

"You know whose cock you're grinding on there?" I ask her.

"Conor," she pants, and he shakes his head in disbelief, but then he takes full advantage of the fact he no longer has to try and hide who he is, grabbing her by the waist and pulling her down onto his cock and making her cry out. Liam stands beside me, coating his cock with lube before crawling onto the bed between Conor's legs and close behind Jessie.

Mikey sits on the edge of the bed and watches while I pull the chair closer so I can have a ringside view of the action unfolding too, because the only thing better than fucking Jessie myself, is watching my brothers do it instead.

Liam rubs his clean hand over her back and onto her shoulders, and she shivers with pleasure. His cock nudges at her ass and she sucks in a deep breath as she keeps riding Conor.

"Want me to hold her still?" Conor asks.

Liam nods in response and Conor holds onto Jessie's hips tightly, pulling her down and pressing her body flush against his. "Just until he's inside, Angel," Conor says as he brushes her hair back from her face. She bites her lip and nods her agreement and my cock throbs in my pants at how compliant she is. I hope Conor and Liam fuck her quickly because I might just come watching her.

Liam slides his other hand between her ass cheeks and pushes a finger inside her and she groans as her body arches forward slightly. He adds another and then he slowly thrusts them in and out as he readies her for him, and she sucks in a deep breath as the skin on her neck flushes pink, a sign she's teetering on the edge again.

"She's close, bro," Conor grinds out the words and Liam withdraws his fingers and lines his cock up against her ass. He shifts closer and holds onto her waist as he pushes himself inside her, and the sight of her being fucked by the two of them makes my cock weep in appreciation.

"Who do you think is fucking your sweet ass, Hacker?" I ask her.

"Liam," she pants as he and Conor fuck her in a steady rhythm.

"Sure is, baby," he says in her ear. "I have missed fucking you so much. And now we get to make you come again."

She whimpers as they rail her, and the moment she falls apart around them is spectacular to watch. Her head falls back against Liam and he wraps his arms around her, pressing her back against his chest as he increases his pace until he fills her with his cum.

"Fuck, Angel. Your pussy sure loves an ass fucking," Conor groans as he holds her hips still against him. "I can feel your cum all over my cock."

"Conor," she groans as Liam pulls out of her gently and releases her to lie on Conor's chest.

"I know, Angel," he says soothingly in her ear. "But we're not done yet."

As Liam climbs off the bed, Mikey takes the lube and squirts some into his hand before rubbing it over his cock and taking his twin brother's place.

"Mikey?" Jessie gasps as he lines up at her ass.

"Yeah, Red. My turn now," he growls as he pushes his cock deep inside her with no further warning and she shudders between the two of them.

"You made Jessie's ass nice and slippery, bro," Mikey

chuckles as he starts to fuck her more roughly than Liam just did. I resist the urge to tell him to slow down because we still have more to do, but I remind myself that he knows, and worships her body, as much as I do.

"Mikey. Conor," Jessie pants and shakes her head as her hands run over Conor's chest.

She wants to say something, but my good girl knows that she can't.

"You want to stop, Angel?" Conor asks.

"No," she shakes her head again and lifts her hands, showing him the gloves.

"You want to take the gloves off?" he asks.

"Yes," she nods.

Conor glances across at me, and I nod my agreement. She clearly doesn't need to feel us with her hands to be able to iden-tify who we are.

"You can take them off," he growls, and she pulls her hands free as soon as the words have left his mouth and tosses the gloves onto the floor. She runs one hand down Conor's chest and snakes the other one behind her and around Mikey's neck, pulling him closer to her. He presses his face against the side of her throat and sucks as he grabs her breasts and squeezes. Conor reaches between her thighs and starts to rub her clit and a few seconds later, she is losing control again. She comes with a loud roar of ecstasy, tipping my two brothers over the edge with her. The three of them lie together, a hot sweaty mess of bodies. All three of them sated and spent — for now. Liam grins at me, clearly having enjoyed watching the latter part of the show as much as I did.

I stand up and walk toward the bed.

Now it's my turn.

CHAPTER

THIRTY-SEVEN

JESSIE

Conor and Mikey breathe heavily in my ears and I pant for breath as I lie sandwiched between their two hard, hot bodies. My blindfold is still on, but at least I can touch them now. My whole body trembles and aches and I groan as Mikey slowly pulls his cock out of my ass. He presses a soft kiss between my shoulder blades.

"Love you, Red," he says softly.

I want to say I love him too, but that's not in my list of permitted words, so I simply say his name and he kisses me again before he pushes himself off the bed. Conor wraps both of his arms around me and kisses the top of my head. "Love you too, Angel," he says, and I wrap my arms around him and kiss his chest. "But you know we're not through yet," he growls as he slides his cock out of me too. A rush of our cum drips between my thighs and I bite my lip as it dribbles onto his groin. He groans as he rolls me over until I'm lying on the bed and I feel him get up and leave me lying alone.

I strain to hear what is happening next. I knew this wasn't over. Shane hasn't even touched me yet, and I still haven't received any punishment — only extreme pleasure. I hear footsteps padding toward the bed and then the sound of Shane's belt buckle before the distinctive whoosh of the leather sliding against the expensive fabric of his suit pants. My heart races even faster and I suck in a deep lungful of air. Another spanking from Shane. So, that's how this is going to end? Despite the three earth shattering orgasms I've already had tonight, my pussy contracts in expectation and the wet heat floods my core.

"You think she needs a break first?" Liam asks.

I assume the response is given non verbally as I don't hear a reply, and I also assume that response is no when I hear Shane's suit pants dropping to the floor and a hushed murmur of voices before someone lies beside me on the bed.

It smells like Shane, but I'm not sure I trust my senses any longer. Whoever it is doesn't speak, instead he pulls me on top of him until I'm straddling him, and I notice he is wearing gloves too so I can't feel his hands. Damn! I would have known for sure who it was then. His cock nudges at my tender pussy and I whimper as he shifts his hips until he is able to push the tip inside me.

"Shane!" I groan loudly.

He doesn't confirm or deny, but as he pulls my hips down and impales me on his huge cock, I know for sure it's him anyway. I bite my lip as I roll my hips over him and a groan rumbles in his chest.

"Fuck, Hacker," he hisses and then his hands disappear from my hips. A few seconds later, he grabs me again, this time minus the gloves.

"Shane," I whimper as he takes full control of my body, pushing against the sweet spot inside me and making me shudder with anticipation and pleasure. The noise of his belt buckle jangling directly behind me distracts me and when I feel the bed dip, I realize someone else is joining the fun. Well, of course they are. Why would Shane get me all to himself when

214

none of the others did? I assume it must be Liam, as Mikey and Conor have only just finished, and although they are machines, they usually need at least ten minutes to recover.

A calloused hand slides over my behind. "Conor?" I gasp.

"Yeah, Angel," he says softly.

"I want to feel you squeeze my cock while you get spanked with my belt, Hacker," Shane growls and I experience an intense fluttering in my core and thighs as my head spins. Conor is going to spank me with Shane's belt? Damn!

I lick my lips in anticipation. He swore he would never do this until he trusted me to know my limits, but I suppose with three of his brothers standing around, he doesn't need to worry so much about losing control. Not that I worry about him doing that. I don't think he could hurt me even if he wanted to, at least not physically.

Conor shifts into place at the foot of the bed and I try to brace myself as much as I can while Shane continues fucking me to distraction.

"Don't be gentle," Shane growls to his brother. "She likes it when you make it sting."

"Okay," Conor replies as he sucks in a breath.

I squeeze his cock involuntarily as he talks about me like I'm nothing to them. Why the hell is this so damn hot? But although his words sound cold, his actions are completely otherwise as he reaches up and pulls me down until I'm lying on his chest. He brushes my damp hair back from my face and kisses my forehead before he wraps his arms around me. "The first one is coming in a few seconds, sweetheart," he whispers in my ear.

I nod against him and brace myself as the first strike of the belt hits directly across the middle of my ass cheeks, making them sting with heat. I flinch instinctively, but Shane holds me in place. It wasn't particularly hard and I can tell Conor is holding back. The next two blows are just as light and although they leave a pleasant stinging behind, I need more.

"Stop tickling her with it, Con. I told you how she likes it. Our girl is tougher than you think."

Pride swells in my chest at Shane's praise and I wait for Conor's response. He doesn't say anything but Shane sighs and I feel his breath dusting over my hair. "I won't let you hurt her, Con," he says softly and the tears prick at my eyes. I know how difficult Conor must be finding this. He is terrified that he might go too far, but to hear Shane tell him that he wouldn't let him makes me feel so safe and protected.

A few seconds later the fourth blow lands much harder than the first three and I whimper against Shane's chest as the wet heat floods my pussy. "Good girl," he whispers in my ear as he rubs his hands over my back and thrusts his cock deeper into me.

For some reason those words almost tip me over the edge. "Shane!" I groan as the heat from my ass and the sensation of his cock filling me as well as his hands rubbing over my skin almost overwhelms me.

"You feel so good on my cock, Jessie," he growls so quietly that I'm sure I'm the only one who can hear him. "I'm going to bury myself inside you every chance I get for the rest of my life. You got that?"

"Yes," I groan.

Conor brings down the belt down again, even harder than the last time, and I press my mouth against Shane's neck to stifle my shriek of pleasure tinged with pain.

"Damn, Hacker," Shane groans as he pumps even harder into me. "You do love a spanking, don't you? Your pussy is milking me so hard, sweetheart."

I can barely form a coherent word as Conor goes on spanking my ass while Shane fucks my pussy. My skin is aflame

216

with heat and fire and I think I'm going to pass out if they don't give me some relief soon. My ass stings like hell because Conor knows how to cause pain, maybe even more than his older brother, but I'm determined to take whatever he can give me. He keeps on spanking my ass with the belt, until my eyes are watering so bad, the tears are running down my cheeks. Shane keeps holding me tight, his arms wrapped around me so I'm pressed close to his chest as he rolls my hips over his cock. Being unable to see sharpens my other senses and I feel everything in high definition, including the tension that begins to creep into his body.

"I think she's had enough, Con," he says but the belt cracks over my ass again, even harder than the last time.

"Conor," Shane shouts, and the sound of the belt dropping to the floor rings around the room.

Shane's hands rub over the tender skin on my ass, soothing the reddened flesh. But Conor obviously hasn't finished and a few seconds later he is behind me again. He leans over me, peppering kisses over my back and shoulders. "Turning your ass red has made me so fucking hard, Angel. You think you can go one more round?" he whispers as his fingers circle my hole.

"Yes," I pant.

"Thank fuck!" he growls as he grabs hold of my hips and pushes his cock deep into my ass in one swift movement, making me cry out his name. Then he and Shane fuck me relentlessly while Liam and Mikey encourage them from the sidelines. I lose count of the orgasms they give me with their cocks and their hands and their mouths on me, but when they finally find their own release, I lie between them, a complete, gibbering, trembling wreck with not a coherent word in my head and I wince as every part of my body aches in the most delicious way.

THIRTY-EIGHT

As Conor slowly slides his cock out of me, I groan loudly. I'm still blindfolded so I can't see anything, but I feel him roll to the side and he rests his hand on my back. The bed dips on the other side of us and I wonder if Mikey or Liam, or both, of them have joined us too. My skin tingles with electricity and every part of my body is hypersensitive. Shane holds onto my hips as he pulls out of me too, and the rush of cum that pours out of me makes my cheeks flush with embarrassment. Shane chuckles softly as he holds me tight against his chest. "You've soaked me in cum, Hacker."

"Sorry," I whisper as I rest my head on his chest and draw in shallow breaths as I try to regain at least some of my senses.

Someone unties my scarf and pulls it from my head and I blink in the bright light of the room as Shane cups my chin and tilts my head so I can look at him. "You okay?" he asks.

"Hmmm," I mumble and he lets my head fall back to his chest. But then his arms disappear and he is rolling me off him and into someone else's arms. I glance up to see Mikey's handsome face smiling down at me.

"Let's go get you cleaned up, Red," he says as he walks us

toward the bathroom and it's only then that I realize Liam is no longer in the room. The sound of running water and the smell of vanilla tells me he's running me a bath, and I smile as I wrap my arms around Mikey's neck and snuggle against him.

Liam is standing waiting for me as Mikey sets me down on my feet.

"Are you getting in with me?" I arch an eyebrow at Liam.

"I could do with a soak," he says with a wink as he climbs into the tub, wincing as he lowers himself into the hot water. He's still not fully recovered and his ribs and shoulders still ache when he exerts himself. When he is sitting comfortably, he holds out a hand to me and I take it, while Mikey holds onto my other one as they help me into the water too. The steam and the heat are making me feel even more lightheaded, and it's a relief to sit down. Liam pulls me between his thighs and I lean back against his chest.

"You not joining us?" I ask Mikey, who perches on the edge of the tub.

"I'm not sure the three of us in there would be all that comfortable, Red," he says with a chuckle. "Besides, I'm going to get us some refreshments. I think we could all use some fluids."

"Red Gatorade for me," Liam says.

"Blue for me please," I add.

"You'll both get whatever I can find," he says with an eye roll, but we both know he'll get us exactly what we asked for. He leans down and gives me a kiss on the cheek before disappearing out of the door, leaving Liam and me alone.

Liam pulls my hair back and kisses my neck softly, and I close my eyes and sigh with contentment.

"You were incredible tonight, baby," he says, his lips grazing my ear and making a shiver run the length of my spine.

"You were pretty incredible yourself. Are you feeling okay?"

"Better than ever," he growls as he wraps his arms around my waist and pulls me close to him until our bodies are sliding together in the bubble filled water. "I'm just sorry I couldn't fuck you for longer."

"It was all perfect."

"Doc says I'll be back to full strength soon." He bites my earlobe. "And then you and me have some serious catching up to do, baby because it damn near killed me having you lying next to me and not being able to fuck you the way I want to these past few weeks."

"Well, I can't wait," I giggle as he rubs his beard over the delicate skin of my neck, tickling me until I squirm in his arms. "It's not exactly easy for me either. I mean, you're pretty hot, Liam Ryan."

"Jessie," he growls my name, and then he reaches for a washcloth. "Let's get you cleaned up before you give me another boner. Because if you do, I'll have to turn you around and make you ride me. Do you want me to wash your hair too?"

"No, it's okay. I'll wash it in the morning."

"Okay," he whispers as he runs the washcloth down my body, over my breasts and stomach and then between my thighs before he proceeds to gently wash my most intimate areas. Considering he is the biggest, and probably the meanest looking of the Ryan brothers, he is by far the most sensitive and gentle. He makes me feel so cared for and suddenly I'm over-come with a rush of love for him.

"I love you, Liam," I breathe as the emotion sticks in my throat.

He drops the washcloth into the water and wraps those huge biceps around me again. "I love you too, Jessie."

"Thank you for tonight. I can't say it was much of a punish-ment though?" I turn my head and arch an eyebrow at him.

"Well, that's because it wasn't supposed to be, baby. Why

punish you when it's much more effective to show you what you'd be missing if you ever left again."

"I never will. You know that, right?"

"Yes." He presses a soft kiss against my temple as Mikey walks back into the room carrying refreshments. Red and blue Gatorade, just like we asked him for.

AFTER I AM THOROUGHLY clean and extremely exhausted, Mikey helps me out of the tub and grabs a huge fluffy towel to wrap me in as Liam hoists himself out too, stifling a groan as he does.

"You sure you're okay?" I ask, stifling a yawn.

"I'm fine." He rotates his shoulder and winces. "Nothing a good sleep won't fix."

"He's trying to get another week off work, Red. Don't mind him," Mikey says with a wink.

"Asshole," Liam fires back good-naturedly.

Mikey rolls his eyes. "Some of us have to go pull an eight hour shift in half an hour."

"I'd say my heart bleeds for you, bro. But I nearly fucking died two weeks ago," Liam says as he starts to dry himself off with a towel. "Hanging on by a thread, the doc said."

Mikey dries me off too as he banters with his twin. "Fuck's sake! How long are you going to dine out on that? It's been two weeks, bro. I'd have been back to work the next day."

Liam laughs out loud. "You took two days off because you hurt your toe last year."

"It was broken. After you dropped a fucking barbell on it!" Mikey protests.

"Boys," I laugh. "Stop arguing. You're harshing my mellow."

"Harshing your mellow?" Mikey raises an eyebrow at me. "Who the fuck says that, Red?"

"What? People used to say that." I open my mouth and feign my indignation. "It's cool."

"No. It was never cool. I'm pretty sure that even when it was cool, it wasn't cool," Liam laughs as he wraps his towel around himself and steps toward me. He bends his head low and presses his lips against mine while Mikey finishes drying me with the towel before he starts to rub arnica oil over my ass cheeks.

"That feel good, Red?" he chuckles and I groan into Liam's mouth. When he has finished, Liam breaks our kiss and Mikey pulls one of his clean, soft cotton t-shirts over my head.

"All done and ready for bed, Red," he whispers in my ear.

"Thank you both," I whisper.

"You're welcome, baby," Liam says with a wink before he and Mikey leave me alone in the room.

As I walk out of the bathroom a few moments later, Shane is pulling back the covers of the freshly made bed.

"You changed the sheets?" I say with a smile as I reach him.

"Well, the other ones were soaked with champagne and cum, sweetheart," he says with a grin as he pats the bed and indicates that I should get in.

I climb in and he pulls the covers over my body before sitting down beside me. "Are you tucking me in?" I grin.

"Sure am. You look beat," he says as he brushes my hair back from my face.

"I am." I stifle a yawn.

"You should count yourself lucky that I care about my brother so much, Jessie," he says with a groan.

"What do you mean?"

"I mean that Conor is taking a shower right now, and it's his turn to spend the night with you. So, I'm going to walk out of here and let him have you all to himself."

"But why should I count myself lucky that you're leaving?" I frown at him. I wish he wouldn't talk in riddles when my brain is already feeling like cotton candy.

"Because," he licks his lips and bends his head low until his mouth is resting against my ear. "What we all just did was incredible and you've got me all fired up, sweetheart. So, if I was to climb into that bed with you, I would spend the whole night doing very, *very* bad things to you."

Despite the many orgasms he and his brothers have given me tonight, and the fact that I don't think I could take any more of them, my insides still flutter at his words. "What kind of bad things?" I purr.

"Don't, Jessie," he growls.

"What are you going to do instead, then?" I murmur.

"I'm going to take a very cold shower and then I'm going to do some work," he says as he sits up.

Reaching up, I brush a lock of hair from his forehead. "You work too hard. You were supposed to be having the night off. We were supposed to do movie night."

He winks at me. "Doing you was much better."

Damn! He is so freaking hot. "Smooth talker," I say with a yawn as my eyelids flutter, heavy with sleep.

"Hey!" he says sharply, and my eyes snap wide open.

"Yeah?"

He brushes the back of his knuckles over my cheek. "No more guilt or feeling bad over mistakes we've made in the past. Okay?" he says with a frown.

"Okay."

"I mean it, Hacker. It's done."

"Have I ever told you how much I love you?"

"No. Tell me," he grins.

"I love you more than candy," I whisper as my eyes close again.

"Candy, huh? Damn, Jessie! That's some deep shit."

"Hmm," I mumble.

He laughs softly and then he leans down and presses a soft kiss on my forehead. "I love you too," he whispers and then he stands and leaves the room and I'm too tired and content to ask him to stay a little longer.

I MUST HAVE DRIFTED off because I'm woken by someone climbing into bed with me. I smile sleepily as Conor presses his body against my back and runs his hand over my hip.

"You okay, Angel?" he asks as he nuzzles my neck.

"Yes. I am deliciously achy and completely spent. I feel like I'm about to have the best night's sleep of my life," I purr as I stretch.

"Come here," he growls and I turn around and allow him to pull me onto his chest, where I snuggle against him as he wraps me in his huge arms. His hand skims my ass and he sucks in a breath. "Damn, Jessie. Why the hell aren't you wearing any panties?"

"Because you bruised my ass, Conor Ryan, and now it's covered in Arnica oil."

"I'm pretty sure you can still wear panties. What the fuck are you trying to do to me, Angel?" he groans.

"You can't seriously be good to go again?" I yawn as I close my eyes and wriggle myself even closer against him.

"Does it hurt?" he asks softly.

"No. I loved it. All of it," I sigh contentedly. "And I love you. You could never hurt me."

He doesn't answer me and I lift my head to look at his handsome face to find him staring into space. "Did you enjoy it?" I ask.

"Yes," he growls as he squeezes me tighter. "Too fucking much. I'm already thinking of all the filthy things I can do to you while you're tied to my bed. We're going to be doing so much more of that, Angel. But you never told me to stop."

I kiss his chest and then press my cheek against him. He's right. I'm not sure when I would have asked him to stop if Shane hadn't intervened, or whether I would have asked at all. I can't get past the feeling that I'd be somehow admitting defeat if I did. I want to take everything he can give me. "I trust you to never hurt me, Conor," I whisper as I close my eyes and listen to the sound of his steady heartbeat thumping against my ear as I drift off to sleep.

THIRTY-NINE

"Jessie," Conor says softly as he gently nudges me awake. "We need to get up, Angel."

I blink in the dark room. Surely it's not morning already? I feel like I've barely been asleep for a few hours.

As I open my eyes, I see Mikey sitting on the edge of the bed with a serious expression on his face. "What's wrong?" I ask as I sit up.

"Shane needs to see us all," Mikey replies.

"Is everything okay? Is it Liam?" I ask as my heart starts to race.

"Liam's fine. Shane just called me down at the club and asked me to come up and wake you guys when I got here. I don't know what's going on," Mikey says.

"I've got a good idea," Conor adds with a sigh as he sits up, taking me with him. He presses a kiss against my temple. "Can you go get Liam, Angel? And meet us in Shane's office?"

"Yes. Of course," I say as I blink at him, still groggy from being woken from a deep sleep, before I climb out of bed.

Mikey takes my hand as I pass him and lifts it to his lips, dusting them lightly over my knuckles. "Thanks, Red."

. . .

I WALK along the hallway to Liam's room, wondering what's so urgent that Shane has pulled Mikey from work and woken the rest of us up in the middle of the night. My stomach twists itself into a knot as I run through the possible scenarios in my head. If all four brothers are in the apartment, then at least I know they're all safe, so what the hell is it?

I open the door to Liam and Mikey's bedroom and can't help but smile at Liam's sleeping form. He lies on his back with his arms above his head and his beautiful, tattooed torso on display as his covers rest just beneath his abs.

Walking over to the bed, I sit beside him and place my hand on his chest, my fingers flexing over the hard muscles. "Liam," I say with a gentle nudge and he groans softly.

"Liam," I say louder and he stirs until he's looking up at me.

"Hey, baby," he smiles sleepily. "You miss me?"

I roll my eyes. "Shane wants to see all of us."

"Why?" he asks, his handsome face pulled into a frown.

"I'm not sure. Everyone is okay, though. Mikey and Conor are in his office waiting for us."

He sits up quickly, throwing the covers off himself.

I SIT on the sofa between Conor and Liam while Mikey hovers nervously near Shane's desk as he watches his eldest brother pulling a bottle of Midleton, Chapter One, out of his bottom drawer. I swallow hard. That is a forty thousand dollar bottle of whiskey, the kind you drink on very special, or very sad occasions.

As soon as Conor sees the bottle, his entire body tenses. Lifting his arm, he reaches behind me and places his hand on Liam's shoulder. There are five crystal tumblers on Shane's desk, and we all watch in silence as he pours a generous measure into each one. When he is done, he nods to Mikey, who passes a glass to each of us on the sofa and it's only when we are each holding a drink that Shane finally speaks. "Patrick Ryan died two hours ago," he says as he looks between his three younger brothers. Then he raises his glass in a toast. "May the evil cunt rot in hell for all eternity."

"For eternity," Mikey echoes before we each down the expensive whiskey. The brothers down theirs in one gulp while I take two. Mikey slams his glass down onto the desk. "Cunt," he mutters under his breath.

Conor has his eyes closed and his fist clenched as he keeps one arm behind me with his hand on Liam's shoulder. Liam stares into space while Shane sits back in his chair and rubs a hand over his jaw. The room is thick with tension and emotion and I can think of nothing else to do other than sit here with them and let them feel whatever it is they need to. I place one hand on Conor's thigh while I reach for Liam's hand and he entwines his fingers with mine, squeezing softly and then we all just sit there quietly.

It's Conor who eventually breaks the silence. "I'm not going to his funeral," he spits.

"I know," Shane replies softly.

"Me neither," Mikey snarls. "I'm never setting foot in Ireland ever again." He looks over at Liam, who nods his agreement.

"I know," Shane says again with a heavy sigh. "But I'll have to go. I need to sort out his estate. And..." he shakes his head and pours another shot of whiskey.

"One of us needs to," Conor finishes for him. "If only to make sure that the fucker is really dead."

"Exactly," Shane replies before he downs another shot.

"You can't go on your own," Conor shakes his head.

"I'm not planning to. Erin will be coming."

I tense instinctively at the mention of her name. Despite the circumstances, I hate that she's going to Ireland with him.

Conor reaches across and squeezes my thigh as Shane looks at me and I swallow, wondering if he noticed my reaction and whether it's going to be an issue. I promised him I'd let the Erin thing go, but I can't help how the thought of him and her alone together makes me feel.

"The ice queen?" Mikey snorts. "You might as well be going alone."

"Well, I was also hoping for some warmer company too," he replies, still looking at me. "You fancy a trip to Ireland, Jessie?"

"Me?" I blink at him.

"Yes," he frowns.

My mouth is suddenly incredibly dry. This seems like a big thing for us, but there is only one answer to his question. "Yes. Of course I'll come with you."

"How long will you be gone for?" Conor asks.

"A week. Maybe. Ten days, tops," Shane replies.

"Fuck!" Mikey hisses. "Ten days? You make sure you look after our girl if you're taking her there, Shane."

"I will," he frowns.

"I can look after myself," I remind them.

"We know," Conor whispers as he kisses my cheek. "You make sure you take care of our boy too," he whispers in my ear.

"I will," I whisper back.

"When are you going?" Liam asks.

"Tomorrow afternoon. There is no rush to get there before then." Shane replies.

"You taking Alejandro's plane?" Conor asks.

"Yes," Shane replies.

"Who is Alejandro?" I ask with a frown.

"A friend of ours," Conor replies. "You'll like him."

"And he has his own plane?"

"He has two," Shane says as he downs another shot of whisky.

"Wow! So we're going to Ireland on a private jet?" I ask.

"Yep," Shane nods.

"It has a bedroom and everything." Liam turns and grins at me.

"Nice!"

"Family dinner tonight, then?" Mikey says.

"Will you make a huge turkey dinner?" Liam asks. "Like with all the trimmings?"

Mikey walks over and ruffles his twin brother's hair. "With every trimming there is, if that's what you all want?"

"Like Thanksgiving in July?" I offer.

"Hmm. If we celebrated Thanksgiving," Liam says.

"You've never celebrated Thanksgiving?" I open my mouth in surprise.

"We're Irish!" Mikey frowns at me.

"But you live in America! How have you avoided like the second biggest holiday?"

"We're usually working," Conor shrugs.

Mikey sits on the arm of the sofa next to Liam. "Thanksgiving in July it is then. You going to help me out, Jessie?"

"Yes," I smile. I love to cook and Mikey has been teaching me so many new dishes. It will be nice to teach him a few traditional American ones.

"It's a date then. Dinner at eight before Shane and Jessie go to Ireland to spit on Patrick Ryan's grave," Mikey declares.

CHAPTER

FORTY

CONOR

A s I watch Mikey, Shane and Jessie carrying the steaming trays of food into the dining room, I can't help smiling. Jessie has a huge grin on her face as she places the mashed potatoes and string beans on the table, and Mikey and Shane bicker good-naturedly over who is going to carve the turkey.

In the ten years we've been in the States, we've never celebrated Thanksgiving – not in the traditional sense anyway. It's not a thing in Ireland so it's not a part of our family history or tradition. But Jessie is insistent that we're going to change that this year, so our Thanksgiving in July is going to be our trial run. And so, she has insisted we have a full on traditional Thanksgiving dinner, which Mikey was more than happy to put together, with the help of his sexy, red-headed sous chef. And I can't think of a time in my life when I have ever had so much to be thankful for.

Liam sits beside me. He still has a way to go until he's back to full strength, but he's getting there, and with Jessie's help, his emotional scars are healing too.

Shane sets the turkey down and sits with a satisfied sigh, as though he cooked the bird rather than just carried it in from the kitchen. He squeezes Jessie's ass as she brushes past him and she leans down and rewards him with a kiss. As she takes her own seat, he continues watching her and the smile on his face is like nothing I've ever seen before. The two of them have worked out whatever it was that was keeping them apart, and the change in the apartment, and in our family, is pronounced. It seems like at last we're all in sync and I can't remember a single moment in my life when I have ever felt this content.

"What's for dessert?" Liam groans as he rubs a hand over his stomach and leans back in his chair.

"Pumpkin pie," Jessie says with a smile. "I made it."

"I've never tried that." Liam narrows his eyes at her. "Is it sweet?"

"Very," Jessie replies.

"Won't be the sweetest thing we've ever eaten on this table though," Shane says as he slides a hand onto Jessie's thigh and squeezes, causing Mikey and Liam to groan their agreement while I laugh as Jessie's cheeks flush pink.

"It's Thanksgiving dinner, boys," she admonishes us. "Can we keep it PG?"

Shane leans across and plants a soft kiss on her neck. "Nothing is ever PG with you around, sweetheart."

She turns to me, as though I might be the one who agrees with her.

"He's right, Angel," I say with a shrug. "But as much as I would love to spread you open on this table and eat your pussy instead of your pumpkin pie, I think I'm too full of turkey and potatoes right now."

She opens her mouth in mock horror and swats me on the arm. "Conor!"

"I have to agree, bro," Liam groans. "But I still want some pie."

"Pie now. Pussy later!" Mikey declares, causing everyone at the table to start laughing, which we're still doing a few moments later when the intercom rings signaling someone is downstairs at the back entrance to our building. The one nobody ever uses, because we rarely have visitors, and if we do, they come through the club. Very few people even know about the entrance at the back.

"Who the fuck is that?" Mikey frowns as he grabs the laptop from the cabinet nearby and opens up the security system. As we all look at the screen, it is Jessie who recognizes our visitor first.

"That's Vlad," she says with a frown. "What is he doing here?"

Mikey peers closer at the screen. "Looks like he's alone too."

"Since when did the head of the Bratva travel without a bodyguard?" Shane frowns.

"And more importantly, why the hell is he here?" I snarl. I knew this fucking happy feeling was too good to be true.

"Let me talk to him," Shane nods his head toward the laptop and Mikey presses a button that allows him to speak.

"Vlad. I'm surprised to see you here after our last encounter," Shane says.

"Mr. Ryan. I need to speak to Jessie. Is she there?"

Jessie opens her mouth to speak, but Shane holds his hand up and shakes his head and she remains quiet. "Why do you want Jessie?" he snarls.

"I have something to discuss with her."

"You heard of this thing called a telephone?" Shane snaps as Jessie frowns at the screen.

"It is not the kind of news I want to give over the telephone."

"You come alone?" Shane asks.

"Yes."

Shane nods to Mikey who turns off the microphone so we can speak freely.

"What the hell has made the head of the Bratva come here alone to speak to Jessie?" Mikey asks with a scowl.

"I don't know. But I need to find out," Jessie replies.

"It could be a trap, Angel," I remind her.

"I don't think so. He was so lovely to me when we met in Central Park. Besides, he's alone. And I don't know. I kind of think Vlad is a man of his word. I don't think he's here to start something."

"I've got a bad feeling about this, but it's your call, Jessie. You want to hear what he has to say?" Shane frowns at her.

"I have to, Shane," she says with a shake of her head. "For him to come all the way here?"

Shane sits back and rubs a hand over his jaw before he glances at me. I nod at him because Jessie is right. There is no way we can turn him away when he has something important to tell her.

"You'd better go let our guest in then," Shane says to Mikey with an arch of one eyebrow.

FIVE MINUTES LATER, the head of the Bratva is sitting at our dining table eyeing the remainder of our Thanksgiving feast, but as we're not sure yet why he's even here, he hasn't been afforded any of our Irish hospitality.

Jessie sits between me and Liam, while Mikey stands behind us and Shane sits to our left. He leans back in his chair, allowing Jessie to do the talking.

"What did you need to speak to me about, Vlad?" she asks.

He glances between me and my brothers, his eyes narrowed in suspicion.

"You can talk in front of them. We have no secrets," she says as she leans forward, resting her arms on the table and I realize she would have made an excellent head of the Bratva. She is tougher than anyone else I know.

Vlad clears his throat before he leans forward too. He seems like he's going to speak, but then he just stares at her and I sense Liam getting twitchy in his seat beside me.

"You look so much like your mother," he finally says.

I hear the breath catch in Jessie's throat, and it makes me wonder whether Vlad has a game plan here. Is he trying to endear to him, or throw her off by mentioning her mom right now?

His eyes dart around the room before he focuses on Jessie. "I've been hearing rumors for a while. I didn't speak of it when we last met, because they were just rumors, and I prefer to deal in facts. But now I have proof, and I thought you should be the first to know."

Jessie visibly trembles in her seat and I take hold of her hand and squeeze reassuringly, although my own anxiety levels have just ratcheted up several notches too.

"Proof of what?" she asks, and the tremor in her voice is clearly audible.

Vlad's Adam's apple bobs in his throat as he swallows, and I know what he's going to say before he opens his mouth, and I'm pretty sure Jessie does too.

Despite that, it still hits me like a truck when he speaks. "The Wolf. He's back."

～

WANT to see what happens next?
Ryan Reign
Ryan Renewed
are available now

ALSO BY SADIE KINCAID

Sadie's latest series, Chicago Ruthless is available for preorder now. Following the lives of the notoriously ruthless Moretti siblings - this series will take you on a rollercoaster of emotions. Packed with angst, action and plenty of steam — preorder yours today

Dante

Joey

Lorenzo

If you haven't read full New York the series yet, you can find them on Amazon and Kindle Unlimited

Ryan Rule

Ryan Redemption

Ryan Retribution

Ryan Reign

Ryan Renewed

New York Ruthless short stories can be found here

A Ryan Reckoning

A Ryan Rewind

A Ryan Restraint

A Ryan Halloween

A Ryan Christmas

A Ryan New Year

Want to know more about The Ryan Brothers' buddies, Alejandro and Alana, and Jackson and Lucia? Find out all about them in Sadie's internationally bestselling LA Ruthless series. Available on Amazon and FREE in Kindle Unlimited.

Fierce King

Fierce Queen

Fierce Betrayal

Fierce Obsession

If you'd like to read about London's hottest couple. Gabriel and Samantha, then check out Sadie's London Ruthless series on Amazon. FREE in Kindle Unlimited.

Dark Angel

Fallen Angel

Dark/ Fallen Angel Duet

If you enjoy super spicy short stories, Sadie also writes the Bound series feat Mack and Jenna, Books 1, 2, 3 and 4 are available now.

Bound and Tamed

Bound and Shared

Bound and Dominated

Bound and Deceived

ACKNOWLEDGMENTS

I'd love to thank all of the wonderful women who have supported me to write this book - my beta readers, ARC reviewers and the wonderful writing community. With a particular mention to TL Swan, Vicki Nicolson and the rest of the Cygnets who are an amazing and inspiring group of women.

I also need to give a special mention to Sue and Michelle who have championed my writing from the outset, and to Kate, for helping make 'that' reunion scene perfect!

To my incredible boys who inspire me to be better every single day. And last, but no means least, a huge thank you to my husband, who is my rock and my biggest supporter.

I couldn't do this without you!

About the Author

Sadie Kincaid is a dark romance author who loves to read and write about hot alpha males and strong, feisty females.

Sadie loves to connect with readers so why not get in touch via social media?

Join Sadie's reader group for the latest news, book recommendations and plenty of fun. Sadie's ladies and Sizzling Alphas

Sign up to Sadie's mailing list for exclusive news about future releases, giveaways and content here

Made in United States
Orlando, FL
14 November 2024

53865427R00150